S0-AWO-500

PUFFIN BOOKS

THE DREAM CARVERS

Born and raised in the Maritimes, Joan Clark lived for over twenty years in Western Canada before returning to the east and settling in St John's, Newfoundland, the setting of this novel. Clark is the author of six books for children as well as fiction for adults, including *The Victory of Geraldine Gull*, which was nominated for the Governor General's Award and won the Canadian Authors Association Award. In 1991, Clark was the recipient of the Marian Engel Award and the Canada-Scotland Exchange Award. *Eiriksdottir*, published in 1994, is her adult novel dealing with some of the same themes and characters as *The Dream Carvers*. *The Dream Carvers* won the Mr Christie's Book Award and the Geoffrey Bilson Award for Historical Fiction for Young People.

JOAN CLARK

The Dream Carvers

Puffin Books

PUFFIN BOOKS
Published by the Penguin Group
Penguin Books Canada Ltd, 10 Alcorn Avenue, Toronto, Ontario,
Canada M4V 3B2
Penguin Books Ltd, 27 Wrights Lane, London W8 5TZ, England
Penguin Books USA Inc., 375 Hudson Street, New York, New York
10014, U.S.A.
Penguin Books Australia Ltd, Ringwood, Victoria, Australia
Penguin Books (NZ) Ltd, 182-190 Wairau Road, Auckland 10, New
Zealand

Penguin Books Ltd, Registered Offices: Harmondsworth, Middlesex
England

First published in Viking by Penguin Books Canada Limited, 1995
Published in Puffin Books, 1997

10 9 8 7 6 5 4 3 2 1

Manufactured in Canada

Canadian Cataloguing in Publication Data

Clark, Joan, 1934–
        The dream carvers

ISBN 0-14-038629-7

I. Title.

PS8555.L37D7 1996   jC813'.54   C94-932582-1
PZ7.C53Dr 1996

for
Anthony

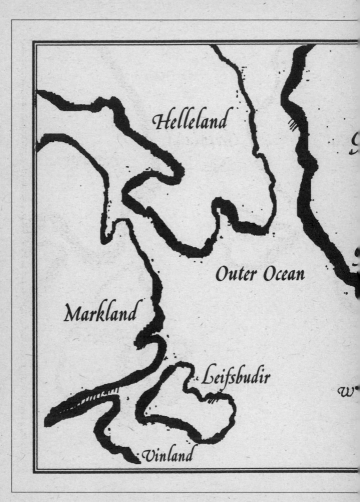

Helleland

Outer Ocean

Markland

Leifsbudir

Vinland

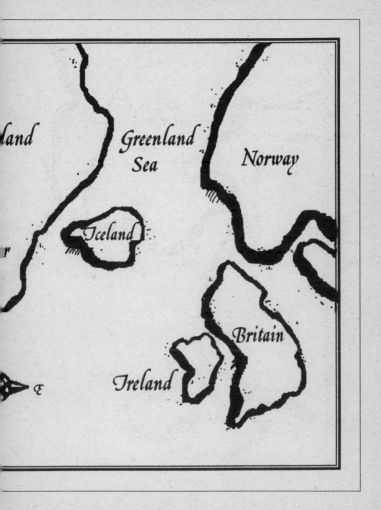

I was an animal, a caribou maybe, or a bear. An animal tied to a pole. The pole, carried by four red hands, bobbed and wove between stands of spruce. Tree spikes pierced my body like iron nails. I was dragged through a thicket of alder whose rough-leafed branches scraped my face. The pole plummeted and my head bumped a large rock. Pain shot from the nape of my neck, crawled under my hair, gripped the sides of my forehead like claws. I closed my eyes, bracing myself for certain death.

I was plunged into water. The water entered my nose and mouth, making me choke and gasp. The pole jerked higher and my body made a furrow across the lake. The lake was shallow and easily crossed. On the other side I was carried through dwarf spruce that slapped and stung. Another lake, but I was ready that time and held my breath while I was dragged underwater. More spruce, brittle and sharp.

We came to a sea. I was loosed from the pole and thrown into a strange red boat. One of the pole carriers sat on my legs and chest. The boat moved away from shore. I looked up at the man straddling me. He had long hair reddened with earth. His entire body was red, as well as his clothes. The other men in the boat were also red. Beyond the red men was the sky, its blueness the colour of summer ice. High above, white clouds were shaped like the backbone of a fish. The sky and the clouds were the only things familiar to me, for I come from a world of blue and white.

The
Dream
Carvers

One

One

1

They have placed me outside their tents where they can keep an eye on me. I notice they took care to stake me in a grassy area empty of anything except myself. There is nothing close by that I can use to cut the bindings that tie my wrists to the stake. The bindings are strips of caribou skin. My feet have been left unbound which means I can move my legs as I please. My captors have cleverly placed a crosspiece at the top of the pole to prevent me from lifting the ties off the stake. At night they take me into one of their tents—there are three altogether—and tie me in a sleeping place, feet toward the fire. In the morning they bring me out here to the stake. For seven days it's been like this. All this time I've been watching my captors, waiting for a chance to escape. And I've been remembering Greenland.

My name is Thrand. I was born fourteen years ago in Gardar, in Greenland. My father owns a farm in the Eastern Settlement, overlooking the fjord. My father is Ozur; my mother is Inga. My younger brothers are Magnus and Erling. Gunnhild is my older sister. My brothers and I help our father with the sheep and cattle; my sister works with my mother dairying and weaving. When my father and I return to Gardar, we will have to work hard to bring in the hay before Winter. The sheep will have to be rounded up and brought down from the pastures near the glacier where they have been grazing all Summer. How good it will be to be home, to taste my mother's blueberry cheese, to eat lamb stewed in angelica, to drink a cup of cold milk. How enjoyable it will be to hear the laughter and jokes of my younger brothers. Before I left Greenland a year ago, I could hardly bear my brothers' childish riddles and games. As the oldest son and the one chosen to go with my father to Leifsbudir, I was swollen with self-importance and pride. What I wouldn't give now to hear one of Erling's silly jokes or to play Magnus's mindless games.

My father and I came to Leifsbudir for wood which is scarce at home. We Greenlanders regard the name of our island as something of a joke since, except for the pastures along the fjords, it is less green than blue and white. There are no trees in Greenland, only rock and grass, water and ice. Alders and osiers grow in the hollows; dwarf birch and juniper survive here and there, but these hardly count as trees since they can't be made into houses or ships. Occasionally enough driftwood comes ashore to make a small rowboat or a bench, perhaps a chest. But wood has to be fetched from forested lands in order to build houses with posts and beams and furnish them with tables and sleeping platforms. At home in Gardar my family lives in a stone hut and sleeps on alder branches and furs spread on the floor.

The year I was born, 1001, Leif Eiriksson crossed the western sea looking for the forested lands and found this country. He built some houses on the edge of the sea about a two-day journey by boat from where I am now, and named them Leifsbudir. That is where my father and I, along with seventy-odd Greenlanders and Icelanders, have been this past year. Mainly we have been harvesting and dressing timber to take back to Greenland. At last my mother will have a fine house in Gardar built with posts and beams. It will have sleeping benches, chests and whatever furniture she wants us to make. Our supply of timber was part of the agreement my father made with Leif Eiriksson's half-sister, Freydis, and her husband, Thorvard, who are the leaders of the Greenland expedition. It was agreed that my father and I would have a share of the wood we helped harvest. For all I know, this wood may already be stowed aboard a ship in preparation for departure. It could be the Icelanders' ship or the new ship built for Freydis and her husband by a Norwegian builder.

Before I was captured, there was some difficulty over which ship we Greenlanders would use for our journey home. Whichever ship was decided upon, it will be loaded and provisioned, made ready for my return. As soon as I find my chance, I intend to take one of my captors' boats—I see two from where I am sitting—and use it to escape to Leifsbudir. If I run into trouble with the boat, I'll go ashore and return on foot. I'm quick on my feet and would make good time along the shore. My escape will have to be soon. My father and the others can't delay their departure much longer without running into ice in Greenland. Late Summer is the only time ships can move in and out of the Eastern Settlement before the fjords become choked with ice. This is the ice that calves from the glaciers covering our island. By late Summer, chunks and bergs of ice, some of them blue with frozen rain water, have sheared off glaciers and tumbled into the fjords, making them impassable to ships.

In addition to a variety of timber, we Greenlanders are taking back a quantity of ivory and rope made from walrus skin, as well as the skins of harp seals and the skins of black bears. We don't have black bears at home, which makes them valuable trade goods for we like to have bearskins on our floors in Winter. In Greenland we have only the great white bears which are hunted with traps on land since they're far too dangerous to be tracked on foot. But this Summer past, we Greenlanders have been tracking black bears in the woods around Leifsbudir.

We Greenlanders were deep in the woods. The other men had treed a large black bear and were waiting for me to throw my axe. As the youngest I was last to be given a bear of my own to kill. Every day I had gone out hunting with the men and watched how a black bear was brought down. By the fourth day out, I had learned enough to be trusted with the kill. Our leader, Thorvard, knew this. That was why he and his hunters were waiting for me to bring down the bear.

I made myself taller by balancing on my toes so that I was nearly as tall as the bear which was upright, its back against a tree. I pulled my arm back as far as it would go. Then I threw my axe putting all my weight behind it. The axe bit into the bear's snout between the eyes. The bear rocked from side to side before toppling in a heap. I watched the dying bear so intently that I didn't see or hear anything else.

Suddenly my eyes and mouth were covered. I was being tilted backwards and lifted off my feet. I was captured so swiftly, so silently that while I was being carried away, the picture of the toppled bear was still before my eyes.

I'm staked on a grassy embankment beside a wide river flowing into the sea. Behind me are spruce woods mixed with birch, ahead is the sea. It doesn't look like a sea, more like a fjord. That's because I'm at the end of a large bay with many islands which make it seem we are inland. If my people were to come looking for me by ship, they would never find me here, since the rocks and shoals would prevent the ship from coming in close enough to see the place where I'm being held.

My captors use boats made of birch-bark. In my view this is short-sighted. Why make a boat from bark when wood is plentiful and sturdier by far? If I could speak to these skraelings, I would tell them how Norsemen build ships. Of course, I can't talk to my captors since they speak a language unknown to me.

Before coming to Leifsbudir, I had never seen a skraeling. In Northsetur far to the north of Gardar where we Greenlanders trap white bears, hunters have seen the occasional skraeling dressed in seal-skin and paddling a skin boat. It is said those skraelings are swarthy, troll-like creatures. The skraelings on this side of the sea appear to be different from the Greenland skraelings. For one thing, they are as tall and well built as Norsemen; for another, they are completely red. They rub their skin and clothing with what appears to be red earth mixed with grease. Their tents are covered with this red powder as are their tools and utensils, as well as the bone ornaments they wear around their necks. Even the boat that brought me here is red. This makes me think I have entered another world. It's true that the sky and sea are blue, the trees and grass green, the rocks and stones grey, but these skraelings seem to inhabit a world of redness where everything they make or use is red. It's as if they imagine themselves living within a red world of their own that's side by side or within the larger world that I know.

As a boy in Greenland I was told skraelings were wretches who lived on the outermost reaches of the world. They weren't people but wild savages who lurked in unknown places. The first skraeling I saw was the thief we killed in Leifsbudir. When I saw him lying near the woods, I was surprised to see how much he resembled me. Now that I've seen many more of them, I know these skraelings eat and sleep and work the way people do. There are men and women, old and young, children and babies just as there are among folk in Greenland. The main difference between skraelings and myself is their redness, at least on the outside. When I return to Leifsbudir and tell my friend Teit how skraelings cover all their goods red, he will no doubt think I'm making up a fanciful story to amuse him. Because Teit was the only Greenlander in Leifsbudir who was close to my age, it was inevitable that we share stories together.

Other than feeding me and moving me between tent and stake, the skraelings ignore me completely. It's as if by not being red, I don't exist. I am outside their world of redness. Except for one. That's the old woman who brings me my food twice daily, usually a roasted fish speared on a wooden stick. She pats my hair and says something that sounds like "Wobee." Over and over, she says this word, "Wobee." I eat the fish because I want to be strong enough to escape. I don't understand why people would feed someone they intend to kill. Do they intend to set me free and then run me down?

The tent where I sleep at night is occupied by the old woman and an old man I take to be her husband. I notice both of them have creased faces, wrinkled necks and move slowly as if from the joint-ill which is how I know they are the oldest people here. The other two tents are occupied by younger men and women and their children, all of them dark-eyed. The hair beneath the red covering seems to be black. It's difficult to know the colour of their skin beneath the red. All of them go about barefoot as well as bare-armed and bare-legged. The women wear some sort of skin tunic, the men a skin hanging from a belt. I myself am wearing skin breeches, a shirt and deerskin shoes. I can see for myself that my hair is light brown and my skin white and sunburnt. I can't, of course, see my eyes but I know that like most Greenlanders', they are more or less blue.

Why have these red people brought me here? Why did they capture me instead of Thorvard or one of the other bear hunters? And why haven't they killed me? This is what a Norseman would do. Norsemen quickly kill whatever is unfamiliar and strange. That is our way. Norsemen sometimes kill each other. It's said that Eirik the Red, the father of Leif, Freydis and their brothers, settled in Greenland because he was banished from Iceland after some killings. Before that, Eirik's father had settled in Iceland after being exiled from Norway for murdering another man. Norsemen sometimes call Greenland the last place on earth, since all too often that is where renegades and murderers come to live.

My father isn't a murderer. He says he has enough difficulty slaughtering cattle and sheep, let alone killing a man. He says the sight of blood makes him ill. At home he hunts only when we need food and leaves the slaughtering of farm animals to me. I have no difficulty killing animals. As for killing people, it's my view that we may kill someone if our survival is threatened. I would kill any man who tried to take what is mine unless, of course, I no longer wanted it. I can't understand why these red people haven't killed me, since it appears that by hunting bear where we did, the other Greenlanders and I crossed into the skraelings' territory and took what was theirs. Perhaps these people dislike killing others. If that is true, they may in that regard be more like my father than I am myself.

2

In my dream I am lost in a forest where everything is red: the trees, the rocks, the lake. Drops of blood fall from a ruddy sky. Moving through the forest are the ghostly figures of people who are completely red, even their eyes are red. They drift through the forest as if it weren't there. They pass through trees and rocks instead of going around or above. They walk on water and fly through the air. These are the undead, the ghosts who occupy an invisible world. I know I'm dead, that I've somehow wandered into a world of red ghosts. I open my mouth and scream.

"Wobee," a voice says. "Wobee."

I open my eyes and see the old woman bending over me. I close them again and return to the forest of ghosts. A ghost drifts through me like red smoke. I shiver from the coldness of its touch.

"Wobee," the old woman says again and smiles. I notice her teeth are white and stumpy, worn down to the jaw. She puts a warm hand on my forehead and rubs it back and forth. I don't want her to touch me, she may be a ghost, but I can't force her hand away since my own are bound. She continues to rub my forehead, all the while speaking her unfamiliar tongue. Does she know how afraid I am of strange forests, coming as I do from a country where trees are scarce? If I could tell her about the ghosts, would they go away? Maybe the old woman understands my fear because after a while, I close my eyes and instead of drifting into the bleeding forest, I lock myself into untroubled sleep.

When I waken again, she's still there, smiling. She pats my head and says, "Wobee," as she does every day.

Today she adds something. She pats her own head and says something that sounds like "Imamasduit." She says this over and over, always patting herself as she speaks. When her husband comes in, she pats his head and says, "Bogodorasook." She does this several times more. I think she's telling me their names and that the name they are using for me is Wobee. I pretend not to understand, though I do. Nor do I tell her my real name. My name, Thrand, which I have taken for granted since I was a child, has become more important to me than it has ever been before, because except for my clothing, it is the only thing I now possess.

Imamasduit takes a skewered fish from the fire and holds it out to me. I elbow myself into a sitting position and hold the stick between my hands. The fish skin is crisp and black from being close to the fire. She watches while I tear the skin away from the flesh with my teeth. I'm hungry but I make myself eat slowly so I can see the bones. I'm halfway through the meal when Bogodorasook beckons Imamasduit outside. After Imamasduit disappears through the tent flap, I reach for a cup of water while trying to hold onto the skewer. To my dismay the rest of the fish slides off the stick and into the fire. No, not into the fire, to one side of it which means that if I can retrieve the fish before it burns, I can finish my meal. I am hungry enough to want to try this. The skewer isn't long enough to reach the fish but there's a large poking stick nearby, to one side of the stone fire ring. My hands have grown clumsy and stiff from being tied—which is why I dropped the fish. But if I can get hold of the stick, I might be able to work the fish out of the stone ring and onto a rock.

I grasp the poking stick between my hands and try to manoeuvre the fish to the edge of the fire. In doing this, a flame licks my deerskin bindings and sears the underside of my wrist. I drop the poking stick and press my wrist against my mouth, using my tongue to soothe the burn. Then I examine my wrist. A welt is rising but it's not very large. The underside of the deer-skin is completely black. I notice a hole in the binding where the flame has eaten through. If I could make the hole larger, I could weaken the binding. Over and over, I hold my wrists close together then force them apart to weaken the tie but this doesn't work. Perhaps I can break the deerskin by rubbing it across a stone. I hold my wrists on either side of a fire stone and rub the binding back and forth. The welt hurts every time it touches the hot stone, but I ignore it and rub harder. Harder, faster. Then I look: the edges of the hole are thinning! I rub and rub, back and forth. I feel the deerskin tearing. Finally it breaks! I'm free! Quickly, I crawl to the tent opening and peer through the flap. No one is close by. I hear voices but they seem to be coming from the woods behind the other tents. Ahead of me is the empty stake. Beyond that, near the water, one of the women is bent over the racks where the fish are being dried, close by the sea. The boats are shore hauled close by the racks. If I can slip between the trees to the right of the tent, I can crawl through the underbrush to the beach without being seen. I hear voices behind the tents off to my left. It sounds as if a meeting of some sort is underway: that must be where the old woman has gone. I'll never have a better chance to make a run for it than now. I crawl through the tent opening, cross the grass and plunge into the woods. Once under cover, I look out. The woman near the water is still bent over the fish racks. Apart from her, no one's in sight. How lucky for me! I lose no time in crawling through the underbrush to the stony shore. The woman has her back to me which means I can creep up to one of the boats and get inside. I flatten myself on the bottom of the boat and wait, willing her to move away.

After a while, someone calls the woman and she

leaves the racks to join the others. Now is my chance. I get out of the boat. Because it's made of tree bark, the boat is light enough for me to lift into the water without making much noise.

The camp is on one side of a fast-flowing tidal river moving toward a bay. On the other side of the bay, opposite the tents, are several large islands which are thickly treed. I intend to avoid these, since reaching them would mean crossing a broad open space where I could be easily seen if my captors looked that way. Instead I paddle close to shore, using the shelter of rocks and trees, heading toward the mouth of the bay where there are more islands. Fortunately, the tide is going out, which means the boat is carried forward with the current despite my clumsy efforts at paddling.

Soon I've reached the end of the river and am well into the bay. The current slows and I paddle harder to make up for the loss of speed. I keep my eye on an island which is further out. Compared to the others in the bay it's small, but because of the lay of the land I don't think it can be seen from the camp. If I can reach it quickly and paddle around to its other side, I'll be invisible to anyone looking out to sea. This is my best chance to outsmart my captors who when they come after me, will likely assume I'm following the shore. Leaning forward, I paddle hard, straight across the bay without looking left, right or behind until I've passed the end of the small island and am on its other side, out of sight of the camp. I stop to rest. My chest heaves and my skin is wet from the exertion, but I'm charged with energy and excitement. A short rest before I continue. I can hardly believe my luck! I notice the small island has birch trees growing on top.

Straight ahead are two large islands with sea birds flying above. In a short while, I'll head for those islands. They are further away than the distance I've come, and to reach them I'll have to cross a stretch of open water that will put me in view of the camp. But once I've made that crossing and am on the other side of the islands, my passage across the bay will be blocked from view. If I can reach the other side of the bay by nightfall, I'll beach the boat and follow the coastline North until I come to Leifsbudir. I pick up the paddle and begin again.

I've barely started the crossing when shouts come across the water from the camp. My captors have discovered my absence! I look at the sea-bird islands. They are steeply cliffed and bare of trees. Even if I reach them, I can see no place to land. Should I take the risk and go on? Already my arms and shoulders ache from paddling this far. My captors are strong paddlers and will have more energy than me. There's no doubt they would catch up to me before I could reach the shore on the other side of the bay.

Reluctantly I turn the boat around and head toward the small island I left behind. The birch trees will provide shelter and hide me until night. When the moon is up, I'll cross the bay. Meanwhile my captors won't know if I'm on one of the islands or if I've beached the canoe somewhere and gone ashore into the woods.

There's no beach on the island. I step onto a rock, pull the boat out of the water, and lifting it to avoid the sharper rocks, haul it into a thicket of alders until it's hidden from view. Bending low, I find the cover of a dwarf spruce and look around. The island rises into a small hill. I climb toward a grove of birch trees on top. A voice reaches me from across the water, on the opposite shore. At the top of the hill, between the birch trees, are mounds of reddened stones. They might be cairns. If they are, they're unlike the high stone markers we build in Greenland. These cairns are low and narrow like graves. Whatever they are, I avoid them, for the reddened stones are clearly the work of my captors, which means this island is being used by them, perhaps as a burial ground.

I've made a mistake coming to this island. I should have taken my chances and kept on paddling toward the sea-bird islands. But it's too late to change my mind. The best thing I can do now is hide here and rest until night when, under cover of darkness, I can continue my escape.

Near the birches is a large spruce whose lower branches are so heavy and thick, they lean on the ground. The branches overlap each other in such a way that they could cover my body completely. I flatten myself beneath the branches where they are thickest.

The ground is damp, fragrant with the smell of spruce needles. I lay my cheek against the needles and try to loosen the fear gripping me. It's no use. As long as I'm being hunted, my body will be as tight as a bowstring. Now that I am lying down, weariness overtakes me. My limbs have become so heavy, I feel I will never be able to lift them again.

The air is windless, empty of all sounds save the cries of distant sea birds. After a while, I hear a light splashing noise. It could be the lapping of a wave against a rock. There it is again! I listen closely. The splashing continues, even, measured. My pursuers are paddling past! I'm sure of this though I can't risk crawling out to look. I lie beneath the branches, still and tense. After a time, the splashing ceases and my body loosens somewhat. My pursuers have moved on.

All afternoon I lie on my belly beneath the spruce. Most of the time I hover between wakefulness and sleep, not daring to sleep lest my pursuers return. Apparently there are no birds or game on this island for I hear nothing close by except shufflings and stirrings of what I take to be mice.

At nightfall, a light breeze disturbs the trees. The leaves of the birch trees rustle. Above me the spruce creaks. I have never been near trees at night and am uneasy with the sounds. I turn over and lie on my back so I can move the branches and look about. It's too early for the moon, but far away I see the flickering stars. I close my eyes and doze while around me the birch leaves flutter and shake. Deep inside its trunk, the spruce groans. Unwillingly I slip into a dream.

All around me are talking trees. I've been captured by forest giants who can see through their skins. Every leaf and needle is an eye. The long arm of a spruce reaches down and presses my arms and shoulders to the ground. I try to get up but I'm unable to move. Needles prick my arms and legs.

Tree fingers grope across my face. The fingers are wet and red. A drop of blood splatters my forehead. Above me, the spruce sways and groans like a grieving ghost.

The spruce has me pinned to the ground. I can feel tree roots creeping over my skin. They are circling my ankles and wrists, binding them tight.

I hear a whisper. It's as faint as the water shifting against the shore but shaped like a voice. It seems to be coming from inside a mound of reddened stones. Within the mound is a severed head. The head is talking to me.

"Wobee," the head whispers, "you killed me."

Whose head is it?

The spruce giant tightens its grip on me. Fingers cover my nose and mouth. I can scarcely breathe.

Above me in the sky the stars are red.

3

An insect crawls up my leg and wakens me. I reach down and slap my leg. My forehead is covered with sweat. I lift my hand and wipe it off. Then I begin to wriggle out of my hiding place. I've been lying still so long that my legs are prickly and stiff. I stand and look at the flickering stars and the rising moon. The moon is halfway up the sky which means it's time to paddle back to Leifsbudir and the people I know. I avoid the mounds and slip between the birches instead. The trees are whitened by moonlight but still they frighten me. As I pass them, their branches reach and grab. The trick is to keep moving so they can't get hold of my arms and legs. I move quickly though noisily, crushing twigs and leaves beneath my feet. The roughness of these sounds reassures me, makes me feel forceful and alive. I come to the rocky shore and stare across the water at the sea-bird islands. The moon has laid a glittering path between them and me. All I need do is follow it, paddling North, past the islands until dawn brings me ashore. From there I'll continue on foot to Leifsbudir.

I push the alders apart, looking for the boat. I know

I hauled it a short distance from the water into the brush. The boat isn't where I thought it was. Maybe in my haste to hide myself, I didn't pay close enough attention to where I was putting it. I continue to search the alder thicket.

There is nothing stranger than a person's thoughts. At what moment did I know for certain that the boat wasn't there, that it had been moved? Who can say how much time went by before I knew? I knew even before the loop swung through the air from behind and fell over my head. I knew before I heard the bird whistle.

Angry words. A noose tightening around my neck. A shout, a command. The noose slackens. A boat appears, from nowhere it seems. Ghostly shapes appear, whitened by moonlight. Someone binds my hands from behind and leads me to the boat. I get in and sit down. One of my captors pushes me onto my back with his foot and sits on my chest. He thumps up and down, forcing out my breath.

"Zathrasook!"

The thumping stops.

I hardly care. Now that my escape has been thwarted, my comfort is neither here nor there.

I'm taken back to the camp and tied to the stake. This time my feet are bound as well. The noose remains around my neck. Once I'm secure, my captors disappear into their tents, leaving me alone in the moonlight. I slump forward, my head between my knees. I've lost all hope of reaching my father or returning home. It's hard for me to think of my father waiting for a son who cannot return. I prefer not to think of my father's despair, for thinking of it only increases my own. But I'm unable to banish the picture of my father from my thoughts. I see him waiting on the moonlit beach of Leifsbudir, lifting his head to look first eastward along the shore, then southward across the meadow, knowing that if I escaped I could return either way. Because I am a fast runner, he knows that if I were on foot I would return by the meadow. If I were using one of my captors' boats, I would come along the shore. My father has never seen skraeling boats but with so much water and wood hereabouts, he is bound to conclude such boats exist.

Anchored in the bay in front of my father is the ship that will take the Greenlanders home. The ship has already been loaded with timber. Tomorrow the provisions will be stowed, as well as the sleeping and cooking gear. The cow will be taken aboard and tethered to the mast.

By now my father will have spoken to Freydis and Thorvard about delaying the voyage a few more days, in case I should return. Neither one will have agreed to this. Freydis will have told my father that she had left a son in Greenland and understood how hard it was for him to leave me behind. She will have reminded my father that the Icelanders had put so many obstacles in the way of the Greenlanders' departure from Leifsbudir that to delay the voyage further would endanger all their lives, it being so late in the sailing season. Even now, some Greenlanders might not be able to reach their farms before Winter, since the Greenland fjords are already freezing over.

My father knows this. Even so, the thought of returning home without me is almost too much for him to bear, for just as I am thinking of his distress, he will be thinking of my mother's, my sister's and brothers' distress as they wait for us in Greenland. My father also knows that once the Greenlanders leave this side of the water, if I'm alive—and he will doubt this I'm sure—my life will be in the hands of strangers. Whether I'm dead or alive, my father knows that once he boards the ship and leaves for Greenland, the odds are that he will never see me again.

Some people are born unlucky, so my mother says. They are born with limbs that break at birth and heal useless and crooked. Others are born dull-witted and cannot speak a sensible word. But I was born healthy with all my wits. My mother also says that some people attract bad luck the way meat attracts maggots. She says that to keep yourself from becoming tainted, it's better to avoid those whom the gods have made unlucky. The gods, three sisters, Being, Necessity and Fate, sit at their loom beneath the Tree, weaving the lives of ordinary people. So my mother says. Whether you are on the good side or the bad side of the gods depends on Chance. If the sisters weave you an unlucky life, there's little you can do to change your fate. Not even Thor can help you out. That's why some folk die from a wound or an amputation that others survive. That's why some people starve to death while others have more than enough to eat and drink. That's why some people are carried off by skraelings while others remain free to continue their way. Until now, I've thought myself a lucky person. Now I think otherwise.

I don't even notice I'm shivering until someone places a caribou-skin robe over my shoulders. Nor do I notice the dryness of my throat until a cup of water is held to my lips. Then I drink until the cup is empty, so great is my thirst. I didn't know my cheeks were wet until a hand wiped them dry. Now the same hand is rubbing grease on my chafed neck where the noose was jerked tight. The hand is gentle and steady. All this time I keep my head down, having no reason to do otherwise. When I eventually look up, I see Imamasduit kneeling beside me. With one hand she holds a cup, with the other she rubs my neck. There's a huge sadness in the old woman's eyes. I've seen it in my mother's eyes when she's sorrowing for other folk. Imamasduit says nothing, but leaves as quietly as she came. How softly these people move. How still they can make themselves for long periods of time.

As a farmer's son I haven't had to be quiet, but when I went hunting with Thorvard in the woods around Leifsbudir, I had to be silent. Thorvard said that to be a good hunter, I must learn to be quiet, to wait patiently so the animals would come to me. But what good is patience now? What am I waiting for? My luck can be no worse than it is now. I understand the truth of the matter which is that my father has no choice but to abandon me, and in so doing put all his hopes for me in the hands of the sisters who are weaving my fate. But what if the sisters sitting beneath the Tree have no power over what happens inside this world of red? Does that mean I have been abandoned by the gods themselves, that from now on I must live without a fate?

4

In the morning Imamasduit brings me a roasted fish but I refuse to eat. If I can't escape, what's the point of being strong? In any case, I've no appetite for food. The old woman takes my face in her hands and lifts it to hers. "Wobee," she says and shakes her head. Her forehead wrinkles in the way my father's does when he's confused or distressed. Imamasduit doesn't seem angry at me for trying to escape. If anything she's more gentle and patient with me than she was before. "Wobee," she says over and over then leaves me alone. I put my head between my knees and stare at the ground.

I don't know how long the girl has been sitting there. I didn't hear her approach. But I know when I look up and see her that she's been there for some time. Once again, I am convinced that my captors live in a different world from mine. There's an invisible wall between us which is why they can move about without my hearing them.

One of the silly games my brother Magnus likes to play with anyone patient enough to sit with him is Stare Me Out. In this game, two people cast a spell on each other by locking their gaze until the loser breaks the spell by looking away. This is the kind of game the girl seems to be playing with me now. Though she isn't giggling the way Magnus does, I refuse to play. I can't avoid stealing glances at her all the same. She's sitting hands clasped around her bended knees. She's wearing a tunic trimmed with what looks like pieces of bone and has a bone ornament around her neck. Like the others, she's covered with red earth, which gives her a sharp, bitter smell. I can see that beneath the covering her features are pleasingly shaped.

Is this creature human? Grandmother says he is. It's true that except for his white skin and blue eyes, the one she calls Wobee looks human, which is to say he has two arms, two legs and a head with two eyes. But some spirits are said to shape themselves into humans and Wobee could be that kind of spirit. Grandmother insists Wobee is human. She says creatures with white skin can be human. Wobee was one of several white men who were recently hunting bear in the woods to the North of us. She reminds me, as if I needed reminding, that there were many more white men in the place of the ice seals where my brother, Awadasut, was killed. Grandmother says that if Wobee had been a spirit, our hunters wouldn't have been able to capture him and bring him here to replace Awadasut.

Wobee can never replace my brother. Nobody can. I despise Wobee for killing my brother. I wouldn't be sitting here with him if it weren't for Grandmother's urging. This morning she insisted we talk about Wobee.

"Unless one of us can enter his mind, Wobee won't survive," Grandmother said.

I didn't say that I didn't care if Wobee survived. To speak so would dishonour Grandmother's words. I told her I was deeply offended that our captive had chosen to hide himself near my brother's grave mound across the water on the island of birches.

"Wobee didn't know that the island was a burial ground. How can he be blamed for hiding there?"

I chose not to answer this. I want to blame Wobee for everything—for the water I spilt early this morning, the finger I pricked with an awl yesterday, the ache I have behind my eyes today.

"Being unkind to Wobee won't bring Awadasut back," Grandmother said.

"Wobee was also born of the Creator," she went on, her voice soft as lapping waves. "He's not an evil person, and has more years ahead of him than behind. We must help him become one of us."

"Why must he become one of us?" I said. I did not know until later that I was shouting. "Why can't we send him away to live on his own? That is what he wants, or he wouldn't have tried to escape. Why not give him what he wants?"

"Because we need him to do the things Awadasut

did," Grandmother said. "We must persuade him of this and teach him our ways. That is why you must learn his thoughts. You have been given special powers to do this." Then she added slyly, "Wobee may welcome a young woman inside his head."

So here I am, sitting close enough to Wobee so that Grandmother can see I am obeying her wishes, yet not so close that I can smell his whiteness which is the odour of rancid fat. How pale he is, like a newly dug root. Because of his whiteness it's hard for me to believe he's alive. If I pricked his finger with an awl, would it bleed?

The girl isn't playing a staring game with me as I thought. Each time I've stolen a glance her way, she's made no attempt to lock eyes with me. It's true her face is turned in my direction, but it seems she's looking through rather than at me, and there's an angry, hostile expression on her face. Why is she staring at me like that? Is she trying to put an evil spell on me? In Greenland there are folk who are said to have the evil eye. They have the power to change others' luck by staring at them. That's why we never look an evil spell caster in the eye. As long as we can avoid looking at the evil eye, we can withstand the spell.

After a time, Imamasduit comes out of the tent and stands between us. She looks at the girl and pats my head.

"Wobee," she says.

"Wobee," the girl repeats, her voice hard and clipped.

Imamasduit looks at me and pats the girl.

"Abidith," she says.

I hesitate. The girl's name doesn't sound difficult to say. Perhaps I should try.

"Abidith," I repeat and look at the girl. It's the first word I've spoken since my capture. It sounds strange coming from my mouth.

The girl doesn't smile but Imamasduit does, showing her worn teeth.

I say Abidith's name once more aloud, then over and over, liking the sound of it in my ears.

Imamasduit holds her arms together, rocking them as if she is cradling a small child. Then she points to Abidith, to show me I think that she's her child. This can't be so, for Imamasduit seems too old to be Abidith's mother. But when Imamasduit repeats the cradling motion, I decide she's telling me that Abidith is her daughter's child, for this time she points to a woman who is sitting with a girl not far away. Though younger than Imamasduit, the woman looks old enough to be Abidith's mother.

Imamasduit claps her hands and goes away. When she returns, she gives Abidith a bark container and points at my neck. The girl gets up, loosens the noose and rubs grease on my skin where the rope has chafed. It's bear grease. I recognize the smell. The girl does this without looking at me. Nor do I look at her. I feel awkward around her since I see that she's more woman than girl, just as I am more man than boy.

When she finishes greasing my neck, she hands Imamasduit the container and returns to her sitting place.

Inside my head I say her name over and over. Abidith. Abidith. Abidith.

I ask myself if she has seen as many years as me. Does she have sisters and brothers? I know which one is her mother but which one is her father? By paying closer attention to these people, I should be able single him out. The number of red people here is small, maybe fifteen or sixteen people, no more. Do they live here all the time? Are there others like them close by?

Abidith doesn't seem foolish as young women sometimes are. In that way she reminds me of my sister. Gunnhild is serious and quiet. It isn't that Gunnhild doesn't enjoy a joke, more that she doesn't bother laughing unless something amuses her. She is independent in her ways, a fact I admire now more than I did in Greenland.

I close my eyes, concentrating, forcing myself to reach out for Wobee's thoughts. Wobee is thinking of someone in his country who is in some ways like myself. Perhaps she is a young woman he intends to wife one day. No, it is his sister whom he admires. I push

Wobee's thoughts away. I have no wish to know about his sister.

Wobee's thoughts have been easy to find. Maybe he is human, as Grandmother says. I am surprised how easily some people's thoughts are found while others remain lost. Zathrasook's thoughts, for instance, are seldom found unless spoken aloud. How strange that his thoughts are usually closed to me while Wobee's are open. When he was alive, I was constantly inside Awadasut's thoughts, which is one reason why I miss him so much.

Once again, Imamasduit comes between Abidith and myself. She is holding a cup of water. The cup is made from birch-bark—all of their containers are made from this bark which is reddened. Imamasduit points to Abidith, to the cup and then at me. Abidith gets up slowly and takes the cup. She brings it to me, kneels down and holds it toward me. Before I can lift my hands to the cup, someone comes up behind me and spits into the cup.

"Zathrasook!" Imamasduit scolds. I look around and see him retreating. Imamasduit tips the water out and hurries away with the cup. Abidith continues to kneel, her eyes downcast. I notice a smile on her lips.

Zathrasook despises Wobee for killing Awadasut. Who

can blame him? He and Awadasut were like brothers. They did everything together and were seldom apart. Zathrasook was there when Awadasut was run down while trying to carry a seal to the woods. It was late Winter and our people had been hungry for months. The caribou hunt had been poor and the seals hadn't come to their usual places, which was why Awadasut and the others went North looking for food.

Zathrasook was also there when they captured Wobee a short time ago. He wanted to be the one to kill Wobee.

"I wanted to bring Wobee's head back on a spear," Zathrasook told me afterwards. "But Grandfather wouldn't allow a killing. He said there had been enough. He wanted Wobee brought back alive."

Zathrasook is angry because he was denied the killing. He says he would feel better inside if Wobee had been killed. Sometimes I wonder if I would also feel better inside if Wobee were dead. But Grandfather says more is lost than gained by killing others.

Imamasduit returns with the cup of clean water and gives it to Abidith who lifts the cup for me. This time I make no attempt to take it in my hands but drink while she holds the cup to my lips. The water is cool and sweet. Abidith is so close I can see that the bone ornament around her neck has two crooked lines running down the middle. Between them are connecting lines. I wonder if the designs have meaning.

When I have finished drinking, the old woman takes the cup. Then she smiles and pats both Abidith and myself on the head. I can tell Abidith doesn't like this, for soon after, she gets up and goes away. Despite her strangeness I want her to come back.

I don't see Abidith again until night-time. I'm lying in my sleeping place when she enters the tent. Abidith chooses a place opposite me, on the other side of the fire, but Imamasduit points to a sleeping place beside me. Reluctantly Abidith moves closer but she doesn't look at me as she arranges her bed and pulls the deer-skin cover over her head.

Why must I be the one to lie next to Wobee? Why not my sister, Dysee? Grandmother insists I be the one and I must abide by her wishes. Even Father and Mother obey Imamasduit and Bogodorasook. Ever since I've been a little child, I've been taught that dis-obedience to either my parents or grandparents weak-ens the fragile cords binding our family.

Grandmother says tonight I must try to enter Wobee's thoughts through his dreams, that a person's thoughts are more open to others during sleep. She says Wobee may not know he killed Awadasut and must be told that he has. Unless he knows what he has done, he can never become one of us. So Grandmother says.

5

It's late Winter. A skraeling is running across the meadow behind Leifsbudir. He's carrying a seal stolen from outside our shed. The meadow is thickly grown with osiers and bog laurel in which snow had caught and deepened. This slows down the skraeling's pace.

I'm running in pursuit of the skraeling, steadily closing the ground between myself and him. Already I've passed the osiers and bog laurel and have reached mossy ground.

Behind me, I hear Thorvard shout, "Go as fast as you can. As long as he keeps the meat, we can catch him!"

I force myself to run harder. The skraeling has some distance to go before he reaches the woods. Without turning, the thief drops the seal. Still I give chase. I can tell the skraeling is slowing down. I know I can catch him.

"Stay with him!" Thorvard yells. "You've nearly got him!"

I'm within striking distance and throw my axe. The blow isn't enough to kill the thief, but it stuns him and he falls to the ground.

Soon Thorvard is at my side.

I'm awakened by another dream, one in which I'm running down the skraeling who stole one of our seals in Leifsbudir last winter. At the time it was happening, the chase thrilled me. Now it frightens me, maybe because in my dream everything is red. It's as if I remember that morning through a red cloud. I move my head back and forth, trying to get rid of the cloudiness. I open my eyes but the redness lingers like fog. I look up at the place where the tent poles lean together and see the blue eye of early morning sky. I look at the layers of bark, noticing how evenly sized they are yet how well they fit together. I study the outlines of the sleepers inside the tent. Imamasduit's shape is small and pointed, her boniness evident beneath her deerskin cover. Bogodorasook's shape is long and wide at the top. Abidith's shape is curved and soft. My gaze moves from one sleeper to another and back again, but the dream won't leave me alone. The picture of a skraeling running across a meadow haunts me and against my will my eyes close again. Immediately I see Thorvard's broad axe raised over the skraeling's head.

As the youngest Greenlander in Leifsbudir, I was pleased to have chased down the thief. We Greenlanders are careful to keep our possessions behind locked doors and move swiftly to prevent those who would take them from us. It's true the seal the skraeling took wasn't behind a locked door, but it was stealing nonetheless.

I see Thorvard's broad axe cleaving the skraeling's

skull, severing the head from the neck.

Now there's a voice in my dream. "Awadasut, my brother," the voice says. The voice is high and shrill like death wails I have heard.

I can't be sure but I think it's Abidith's voice. How can that be if she's asleep? I force my eyes open and turn my head sideways toward Abidith. The flap of her deerskin cover has been thrown back and I can plainly see that her mouth and eyes are closed. The voice speaks again.

"Awadasut, my brother, is dead," it says, "He lies in the grave mound on the island of birches." Abidith's voice seems to be coming not from her mouth but from inside my head. How can that be?

"Wobee killed my brother."

I look at Abidith. Her eyes remain closed. Tears course down her cheeks. She weeps and weeps. The tears make crooked lines on her skin. After a while, she puts the flap over her face and moves on her side, away from me.

After this, I cannot sleep for now I know the truth, which is that the skraeling I ran down in the meadow was Abidith's brother. I do not know which is worse: the knowledge of my part in his death, or the fact that I am now lying beside the dead man's sister, and she beside me. Such a thing would never happen in Greenland.

When the sun finally arrives at the tent door, the others get up and go outside. They do this without speaking. Not even Imamasduit speaks to me. Why is this? Is it because like Abidith, Imamasduit thinks I killed Awadasut? Or is it that I interpret her silence differently, knowing that the seal thief was Abidith's brother? Is it my own shame about Awadasut's death that makes me see myself as wrong in these people's eyes?

I didn't kill Abidith's brother, Thorvard did. I merely chased Awadasut down. Why didn't these people capture Thorvard? He was the leader of our bear-hunting expedition. Why are they punishing me instead? Why should I trade my life for the actions of someone else? I now expect these red people will kill me, or at the very least use me as a thrall.

In Greenland we keep many thralls. They are mainly Celts from places like Ireland and the Hebrides. They are usually the children of farmers and fishermen who have been caught unawares by Viking raiders who carry them off to places like Bergen and Kaupang where they sell them to Norwegian traders who bring them to Iceland and Greenland and exchange them for ivory, furs and the woven cloth we call wadmal. My father has a thrall named Glub who helps with farm chores and sleeps in the cattle byre during Summer. In Winter, my father allows him to sleep inside our hut near the hearth. My mother also has a thrall. Her name is Mifelyn. Mifelyn claims she was the daughter of an Irish king before her abduction. When I last saw her, she didn't look like a princess, being old and crippled with joint-ill. Because of Mifeyln's extreme old age—she's fifty-one—she's permitted to sleep inside our hut beneath my mother's loom.

I think about our hut in Greenland, the stone hearth running down the middle, the tools and clothing hanging from the roof, the warmth and crowdedness of the room. I see my brothers shoving and pushing each other until my mother sends them outside to play. I see Gunnhild inside the dairy hut pouring out milk or churning butter, her eyes intent on her work. I see my mother at the loom, weaving wadmal for our winter clothes. Before I left Greenland a year ago, she had promised to make me new breeches and a shirt. Perhaps she's weaving cloth for them now.

It's only by thinking of my family that I can make the memory of myself chasing Awadasut go away. I see my sister in the dairy, my mother at her loom, my father sitting on the beach at Leifsbudir waiting for me. When I think of my family this way, my cheeks grow wet. As I weep, I remember Abidith's wet cheeks and the picture of her dead brother returns. I know that the loss of her brother is wounding to her. But I also have a wound: I've been torn from my family, which in my view is a kind of death.

6

The days drag past. Every morning I am taken outside and tied to the stake then left alone. Imamasduit brings me food and water. She greases my neck, but like the others, she now says nothing to me, not even Wobee.

Abidith no longer sleeps next to me at night. I see her only at a distance during the day, moving about with some task or other. Now that she's gone I no longer dream of Awadasut's death, which makes me wonder if she somehow caused the dream.

One morning ten days after my escape attempt, soon after I've been tied to the stake, Bogodorasook appears in front of me with a knife. His approach is so sudden that I turn my head from him and flinch. Bogodorasook appears not to notice, but removes my noose and loosens my wrist and ankle bindings as casually as if he were untying a boat. He tosses the bindings on the grass and points to a boat in the water. There are three men in the boat, Zathrasook among them. I get to my feet and lurch after Bogodorasook, stumbling frequently from having been bound.

When we reach the boat, Bogodorasook points to the bow and I sit down. He hands me a paddle which slides between my weakened hands and into the water. Bogodorasook retrieves the paddle and places it between my hands. He makes a paddling gesture to indicate what he expects of me.

I look down and see ballast rocks have been placed in the bottom of the boat and covered with sod. I kneel on the sod, one knee braced against the gunwale and prepare to paddle. Behind me Bogodorasook and two other men arrange themselves in the middle. Zathrasook sits in the stern with a paddle. Zathrasook makes a deep cut in the water with his paddle and we move ahead. The boat is sharply keeled which makes it slice the water cleanly. Zathrasook is a strong paddler and shoots us forward with every stroke. I am awkward with my paddle, making clumsy stabs in the sea, but I try to keep up, if only to chase away unwanted fears. Do they intend to abandon me on an island? Will they throw me overboard and make me swim ashore?

The sea is calm today and that, combined with Zathrasook's strength and skill, makes our passage swift. We pass the large treed islands, paddling toward the island of birches where I hid after my escape. From my dreams I know Awadasut's grave mound is on this island, for I heard his voice in my dream. We pass the island without going ashore and continue East, heading toward the sea-bird islands I saw before. By now I've got the rhythm of Zathrasook's stroke and try to match my paddle to his. After being staked for so many days, the bracing air and buoyant water strengthen me. As we near the islands, the sea birds fly around and above us. Mainly they are gulls and murres which are a familiar sight in Greenland. I begin to see a number of black-and-white birds on the rocks. They are erect and tall. If I were standing beside them, their heads would probably reach past my knees. I recognize them at once. They are great auks which we have in Greenland. I remember passing them in Lambeyarsund on our way here. My mother's brother used to bring us great auks when he returned from hunting on the coast. I remember the birds were tender-eating and tasted sweeter than lamb.

Zathrasook manoeuvres the boat close by the cliff. Bogodorasook stands up, clubs one of the auks on the head and the bird tumbles into the boat. The other auk runs into the water and dives. We continue paddling alongside the cliff while Bogodorasook and the others club three more auks. From the amount of bird droppings streaking the rocks, it's clear this is the nesting place of many more sea birds than those we see here. Now that Summer is nearly at an end, most of the sea birds have moved to islands further South.

We come to a rocky cove and go ashore. Bogodorasook hands me a club and I follow the others. I have the urge to run back to the boat and paddle away, leaving my captors stranded here, but the notion is fleeting. These men are strong and swift on their feet. They would bring me down well before I reached the boat. There are about six pairs of auks on

the island. They are handsome birds: black feathers
gleaming on their backs, white circles above their
eyes, curved yellow beaks. I pick out a particularly
large auk and give it chase. It runs croaking, its short
wings at its sides, trying to make the edge of the cliff
before I can bring it down. To my surprise, it can run
as fast as I can. Before I can club it, something hard
hits my skull and I fall into darkness.

When I come to, I am on the bottom of the boat
which is again moving through water. Apparently, I
have been lying here for some time, unaware that the
men went on to hunt more auks on the second island.
Now there's a large pile of auks in the boat and we are
on our way back to camp.

I hear the swish of water as the boat moves
through the sea. There are murmuring voices. A sharp
pain at the back of my head. I try to remember how I
fell. I must have been clubbed, for if I had tripped, I
would have hit my forehead. Maybe one of my captors mistook my pursuit of the auk as an attempt to
escape. Or Zathrasook might have found another way
to spit into my cup.

To distract myself from my wound, I look at the
boat and try to concentrate on how it is made. Its keel
has been shaped by ribs in much the same way our
Norse ships are. In fact, the entire shape of the boat
is somewhat like ours with high curved stems at either
end. Otherwise our boats are different; Norse prams
are made of boards riveted together whereas this boat

is made of tree bark sewn with what looks like tree root. The stitching hasn't been made with deer sinew, that I can plainly see. It amazes me that boats can be made from bark. Though I know little of trees, bark seems too light and flimsy to make vessels. It's obvious this boat was cunningly made to be able to travel through the sea without taking on water. Norse boats leak and must be bailed from time to time, whereas the inside of this boat is dry.

That night I'm brought to the fire outside the tents where the red people sit in the circle and feast on roasted auk. I notice that on some occasions, these people prefer to eat around a large fire outside rather than use their fires inside. Altogether I count sixteen people including children and babies. There are more women and girls than there are men and boys. While they eat, the people talk softly among themselves. I listen, trying to understand the meaning of the words. Other than Abidith's and Bogodorasook's names, the words are a blur of sound. Imamasduit gives me roasted auk on a stick. The meat tastes as tender and sweet as I remembered. Even so, it doesn't agree with me and soon I'm vomiting on the ground. The blow on my head has made me ill. My wound is now swollen to the size of a large beach stone.

I try to concentrate on the people, to sort them into families. Maybe they are all one family, it's difficult to say. I'm so dazed and sleepy, I have difficulty sitting upright. After a while, Imamasduit leads me to my sleeping place. Once I am there, she puts damp moss on my head to ease the pain. Soon I'm asleep.

In the morning, there's a skiff of snow on the ground and the air is cold and sharp. Though my head pain has abated somewhat, and I am no longer bound to a stake, I can no longer fool myself into believing I can return to Greenland this season. I know the Greenlanders' ship will be well out to sea by now. If I try to escape before Winter, I am bound to perish for the simple reason that except for Leifsbudir, I am unfamiliar with this land. The world has many countries, no one knows how many. It is said that learned men have drawn pictures of the world's countries on sheepskin vellum which seamen have used to sail from place to place. They call such drawings "maps." We Greenlanders had no maps to guide us on our voyage to Vinland. Our helmsman brought us to Leifsbudir by using a picture he kept inside his head. The picture was made from Leif Eiriksson's description of various currents and landfalls.

The truth is I don't know where in the world I am. I only know that I am in a country to the West of Greenland. I know nothing of the size of this land, or what people and creatures inhabit it. Only one thing is clear to me now and that is that with Winter approaching, I must wait until next Summer before attempting another escape. Between then and now, I will make every effort to learn from my captors, for it's on them that my survival, however precarious, depends.

7

The first snow melts. It's soon followed by another which also disappears. The swelling at the back of my head has long since gone. I have begun a calendar stick. Every day I make a groove in the stick with a sharp rock flake. It's been a month and a half since my capture. By now my father will be home in Gardar. Besides marking the passage of days in the wood, I carve designs which remind me of my family.

One of the pointed shapes at the top of the stick is the snood my mother wears on her head, the other is my father's grey beard. Below are Gunnhild's eyes which I've carved with their eyelids lowered. My sister often goes about with her eyelids lowered. Underneath this are two open mouths belonging to Magnus and Erling. It cheers me to think of my brothers laughing and talking in their noisy way. Carving these designs takes a long time since I'm not used to working with stone tools. But I enjoy doing it. While I am cutting the shapes into wood, I feel that in some way I'm connected with my family and bettering their luck. At the bottom of the stick, I'm carving the house my father is building my mother. I like to think that as

he works on the house, I'm working with him. As I
carve my house, I'm outside in the Greenland air
which is so thin and clear I can hear the sound of a
cow bell on the other side of the fjord. I hear our cattle munching the grass. I hear my mother, who's
weaving outside, beating down the weft with her
whalebone bat. Every so often, my father calls to her
and she leaves her loom to discuss some detail of the
house. Already the posts and roof beams are in place
and he has started on the walls. I try not to see the
sorrow in my mother's eyes when she thinks about
the absent son who would be helping his father if he
were there.

I also occupy myself by learning as much as I can
from my captors so that I can escape one day. Every
morning when I awaken, I say the name Imamasduit
has given me. Wobee, I say over and over inside my
head, trying to get used to it. It's a much softer name
than Thrand. Then I say the other names I have
learned: Abidith, Imamasduit, Bogodorasook, and
their son, Shawbawsut, who is the husband of
Thoowidith. They are Abidith's parents as well as
Dysee's. Dysee and her husband, Hathasut, have a
daughter of about three years named Messee.

Imamasduit has taught me these names. She no
longer ignores me. Nor does she bring me food. Now I
eat with Bogodorasook and her beside the fire in the
centre of their tent. While we eat, Imamasduit points
to the fish we are eating and says, "baubooshat," until

I can repeat the word after her. Or she points to the birch-bark between the tent poles and says, "boyish." At night when we join the others around the fire, one of the young children comes to me with a handful of berries and says, "bibidigemidic" or "manus," depending on what kind of berry it is. In this way, I am slowly learning my captors' language.

I now know that the sixteen people here are one family. I have learned this from Imamasduit and from closely watching the way they touch each other, the way they look and speak with their bodies, the way the small children run to their parents. I notice that except for Zathrasook, everyone but the youngest children wears some sort of neck ornament. I wonder about this since Zathrasook seems as old as Abidith yet she wears an ornament and he doesn't.

Besides being parents to Abidith's father Shaw-bawsut, Imamasduit and Bogodorasook are parents of Zathrasook's mother Woasut. His father is Boasook. Zathrasook has a younger sister Merooish who follows him around and an older sister named Adensit who is the wife of Tisewsut. They have a daughter about Messee's age named Pugathit.

One morning I draw stick pictures of everyone on the snow, and join them together with lines to show how they fit together.

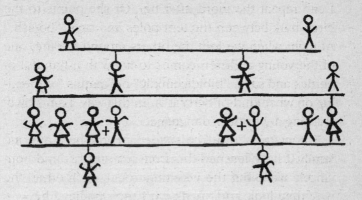

When Abidith walks by, I point to the figures. I
have drawn each one slightly different to show who
they are. I've tried to make the shapes amusing.
Abidith doesn't like what I've done. She takes my
drawing stick and draws a figure beside her own. The
figure is lying down and has no head. Awadasut. Then
she throws the stick aside and walks away. Soon the
snow will melt the figures. I don't wait until then but
erase them with my feet.

Later that morning I make another mistake. I go to
the platform where Dysee is gutting fish. I take a fish
out of the basket and slap it down, intending to slice
its belly. Before I can make the cut, Dysee picks up
the fish and throws it back into the basket. She does
this laughingly and points to the men. She's telling me
to leave her and join the men, that gutting fish is the
work of women, not men. I feel foolish not to have
noticed this custom, or having noticed, not to have

followed it. Collecting birch-bark and firewood is also the work of women. I've watched while men fell trees for firewood. Then they cut them up, leaving firewood for the women to pick up.

I go over to the fire where the men are making weapons and tools. My captors don't use iron tools but cut and whittle tools from rocks of various kinds. We Greenlanders use tools made from iron, sometimes bronze. In Norway, tools and weapons of silver, even gold, are used, but these belong to kings and wealthy jarls, not to ordinary folk. These red people are forever pounding, hacking, chipping rock into flakes, axes, scrapers, knives, spear and arrow points. The men, Bogodorasook among them, sit around the fire outside, patiently turning and shaping rock until it becomes something they can use. Shawbawsut does this with great care; as a result his tools are more pleasingly shaped than the others. I linger close by, watching the men work. I do this as much to be included in their company as to learn how to shape rock. I envy the easy way they have with each other. In Leifsbudir Teit and I enjoyed the same kind of companionship. The men show no interest in being companionable with me and continue to treat me as if I wasn't here. None of them looks at me or speaks. I notice the rock they are using is very different from the rock I know. It's light in weight and is coloured in varying shades of grey and brown. It seems this rock is from someplace else. I haven't seen it in Leifsbudir or close by here. The men keep chunks of this rock in a sack, which means it was likely carried here from elsewhere.

Sometimes I linger near the women as they work around the fire inside, cooking and sewing. Like the men, they say nothing to me, only to each other. They lean their heads together, then look at me and laugh. Oddly enough, this doesn't bother me since their laughter is gentle and not at all unkind. Though I am not included in their work, at least my presence is noticed. Imamasduit chews caribou skin, to soften it I suppose. I have never seen a woman do this before. My mother makes leggings and shoes from deerskin but she has Mifelyn soften it by soaking it in hot water before beating it with stones. Of course, most of our clothes are made from the wadmal my mother weaves, whereas these red people wear clothes of caribou skin.

Everyone in the camp is busy with one task or other. Even the children play in such a way as to imitate their elders. I am the only one who isn't fully occupied. I aimlessly wander about or watch the men, hoping one of them will include me in his work, so that I can make myself useful. During the early days of my capture I had thought that if I wasn't killed, I would be used as a thrall. In Greenland slaves are worked all day, doing the meanest, heaviest chores. Now I find myself almost wanting to be used as a thrall. Anything would be better than being treated as if I were useless.

I know I'm being shunned because of Awadasut, that I'm regarded by my captors as Awadasut's murderer. Perhaps because I've been alone so much, I've gradually come to see that I did play a part in his death. There's no denying I ran him down. It's true I was following Thorvard's orders but that shouldn't have made me blind to choice. After Awadasut dropped the seal, I could, if I had been a different person, have let him go. Instead I threw my axe.

I have relived the chase many times, both in and out of dreams. If I could redream the event, I would. I would redream it in such a way that I would slow myself down and let Awadasut go. But even gods like Odin and Thor are powerless to remake the past, except through tales.

One day, when I am sitting on a log away from the others, I purposely carve my finger to make it bleed. I don't know why I do this. Maybe I feel so useless that I'm trying to prove I'm still alive. Maybe I'm curious as to what will happen next. Maybe I'm willing myself dead instead of Awadasut. I smear blood over one hand until it's red. Then I smear the other. Now I have two red hands. I look up. Imamasduit is watching me. I hold up my bloodied hands for her to see. The carved flesh continues to ooze blood. I smear my arms until they too are red. Imamasduit comes over to me. She urges me to stand and hold out my red hands. Gesturing, she bids me follow her around the camp-site and stop in front of everyone. Each time I stop, the red person looks at my hands then nods thoughtfully. Even Abidith nods. As she walks me from one person to another, Imamasduit speaks to them, saying the same thing over and over again. I don't know exactly what it is, but I think she's telling the others that I've been shunned long enough, that it's time to let me become one of them.

8

Ten days have passed since I bloodied myself. I still don't know why I smeared blood on my skin, unless it was to make myself red. Perhaps despair at my aloneness and invisibility drove me to draw attention to myself in that way. Whatever the reason, it seems to have improved my situation with my captors, for they are now willing to include me in various ways.

It also seems that the season of mourning Awadasut's death has passed, for my captors, who I've learned call themselves Osweet, have stopped looking at me as if I were a ghost or an evil spirit. Now they see me, I think, as someone who is flesh and blood like them.

The men now encourage me to work by their side. I've been given various cutting tools and shown how to use them on stone and wood. I'm making myself a knife with a wide flat blade to which I intend to tie a wooden handle. I have discovered that carving wood gives me such pleasure that this will only be one of several carving tools I intend to make. While I've been working, I've been trying to remember how iron is made. But I can't remember what I never knew.

Although Nagli the ironworker was in Leifsbudir last year, I didn't take the time to inquire as to how he turned bog ore into iron. I know he used charcoal which he made by burning wood. Apart from that, I have little knowledge of what Nagli did. I suppose I didn't trouble to learn because iron ore is scarce in Gardar. Most of the iron goods in Greenland are brought in from Iceland and Norway. I regret not having learned, for if ore could be found in these parts, I could teach the Osweet to forge iron so they wouldn't have to work with stone tools to make what I regard as inferior goods.

Since my capture our main source of food has been salmon.

Now we are eating cod. Twice daily two men go out to empty the nets, usually the same two, Shawbawsut and Boasook. I don't know why this is. There are two boats after all. I can only think that one boat is used because the fish supply is dwindling and only two men are required. I've watched Shawbawsut and Boasook mending the skin nets. It's the only time I've seen men using a bone awl which they store inside a hollow caribou bone.

One morning I awaken to find a bow, four arrows and a spear have been set beside my sleeping place along with a caribou skin sheath and fur-lined boots. Imamasduit and Bogodorasook are sitting near the fire. I can see they have been waiting patiently for me to waken and notice the goods they've made. Because

these gifts are unexpected, I am surprised by the pleasure they bring. To give a captive gifts seems an
unlikely thing. In Greenland thralls are given little but
cast-off clothes. I don't know of any thrall who's been
given gifts his owners have made for him. I am over-
whelmed by the kindness of these two old people. I
examine the arrow and spearheads which are light
brown in colour. The spear and two of the arrows
have been sharpened to very fine points. The other
two arrowheads are blunt: they are for bringing down
birds. I fit an arrow into the sheath and put it over my
shoulder to show Bogodorasook that I know what it's
for. Imamasduit gestures for me to try on the boots.
The caribou fur is thick and soft against my skin.
Since the weather's turned cool, my feet have often
been cold. Now they'll be warm and dry.

It snows again, more heavily this time. Because of
my warm boots, the snow no longer bothers me.
Imamasduit has given me a caribou fur and bid me
wear it over my shoulders as a robe, as she and
Bogodorasook do. These robes have been inside our
tent all along where they've been folded to make sitting places for us. Now that it's grown colder, all the
people are wearing robes.

Several days later, I take my calendar stick and cut
a line through my second month of captivity. The
same morning we begin breaking camp.

For the last two days, we have had to go without
eating fish. Instead the men have gone into the forest

to hunt small game. I myself went into the woods with Bogodorasook. I attempted to kill a large gull but my arrows fell short. Bogodorasook shot two black-backed gulls and these, along with four ptarmigan the other men have brought in, were roasted for our meal that night. It's been clear to me that once fishing stopped, we would have to leave this place or starve. Lacking cattle and other livestock, the Osweet must move to where there is a supply of food.

The sleeping furs and skins are rolled up and tied, our tools and utensils bundled up. The tents are taken down and packed. The tent poles are lashed together at one end as well as halfway down to make a sling for carrying goods. The birch-bark the women have harvested is tied together, wrapped in caribou skin and placed on a platform of boards lashed together with caribou ties. One end of the boards is curved for easier pulling through heavy snow. Watching this, I think how useful it would be to have a sled to carry goods. The platform could be made into a sled by mounting it on skis. Later on, when there's time, maybe I'll try making skis.

These preparations take the morning. By early afternoon our goods are ready for carrying. When the next snowfall comes, the only sign a camp-site has been here will be fire-blackened rocks, the drying racks and the sticks and poles we have used. I remove the stake where I once was tied and toss it into the woods. I expect to be harnessed to the sling of poles since two men will be needed to haul that load.

Bogodorasook gestures for me to follow him to the water's edge. Zathrasook is already there. Two boats, two men. So this is what my work will be. Bogodorasook leans down, grips two crossbeams and hoists them up so that a crossbeam rests on his shoulders. Then he walks a few paces with the boat and sets it down. He gestures for me to pick it up and I do, though not as easily as he. The boat is amazingly light, so different from Norse boats which can't be easily carried. Of course if Norsemen want to travel far, they use ships, not boats. Now I know why the Osweet haven't made wooden boats. It's not that they lack the skill, but that a heavy wooden boat wouldn't suit them half so well. The boat on my shoulders, which they call a canoe, was built to be carried. The fact that we are taking the canoes with us means that we will be travelling through places where canoes can't be paddled, to a destination where boats will be needed.

Bogodorasook and Imamasduit lead the way, each carrying a bundle of skins on their backs. Shawbawsut and Boasook come next hauling the pole sling; their wives, Thoowidith and Woasut, follow, pulling the curved boards. The others fall in behind carrying an assortment of bundles and sacks. We boat-carriers bring up the rear, Zathrasook first, then me.

The snow is well below our ankles except where it's wind-drifted here and there. By the time we boat-carriers reach the drifts, they have been trampled down by those ahead and are easily crossed. We are following the shore of the lake that joins the river flowing into the bay. Both sides of the lake are thickly forested but there's a trail of some sort between the trees.

It's cool but far from cold. Dressed in my robe and fur-lined boots I'm pleasantly warm. Fortunately the air is windless. I can see that a strong wind could make carrying a canoe difficult for it would push the canoe from side to side. I am carrying the canoe on my shoulders, not my back. To keep my neck from being bent, I hold my head inside the canoe which smells of spruce and something else, seal oil I think. Every so often, I tilt the canoe up so that I can see Zathrasook ahead. I don't want to get too close to him lest we collide. On the other hand, I wouldn't put it past him to go ahead so quickly that I'm left far behind. Since I'm following his tracks, he could lead me astray. It's hard to say what he would do to me if he got me alone, away from the others. I continue to expect the worst until it occurs to me that as long as I'm a carrier, Zathrasook won't hurt me for he knows I'm needed to carry the canoe.

We come to a small lake. Here we stop to rest and I have a chance to look around. The lake has begun to freeze from the outside in. The river flows from the end of the lake, toward the sea we are leaving behind. Untying the bark cup Imamasduit gave me before we left, I make my way to the river to fetch a drink. I keep a wary eye out for Zathrasook, but he's run ahead to visit the others and I'm left alone.

It's not long before we're on our way again. Soon we reach the end of the lake where we again pick up the river that gradually narrows into a smaller stream. We follow it along until we come to a second lake. On the south side of the lake we stop beside a round cleared area now filled with snow. This is a tent-site very like the ones we left behind, only three times their size. I expect us to begin making a tent, but no one makes a move to do this. Instead the women and children collect firewood and the men take their weapons and go off to hunt.

By now it's late afternoon and the trees cast long blue shadows across the snow. I'm reluctant to enter the woods alone. At the same time, I don't want to stay with the women. I take up my bow and arrows and follow the men into the forest. I notice their tracks go off in different directions, in pairs. All except one. I follow these. It occurs to me that I could continue walking away and escape. But this is only a passing thought. Escaping in snow would be a futile exercise since the Osweet could easily follow my tracks and bring me back. I would be staked all over again. In any case, where would I go? This land is so vast that without a boat I would be swallowed by its size. I have learned the hard way that if I am to make a successful escape, I will have to plan it well ahead.

I see ptarmigan tracks and follow these. All the while the shadows deepen and merge. The air grows darker. I must remember to follow my footprints back to the camp while it's light enough. But my empty belly pushes me forward after the ptarmigan. I try to walk softly as the Osweet do.

I come upon the ptarmigan suddenly in an open space. Leaning against a tree to steady myself, I fit an arrow and lift my bow. Slow and sure, I say to myself, don't rush and fumble. I pull the arrow far back, farther still. I let it go. Amazingly the arrow hits its mark, piercing the bird through the throat.

Before I can retrieve my kill, an arrow comes from behind me, enters my tunic cloth above the elbow and pins me to the tree. Quickly I duck then look around but no one's in sight. I reach over, across my pinioned arm and wrest the arrow free. It comes away easily. I poke my finger through the tunic hole. There's no hole in my body, not even a scratch on my skin. Even so blood rushes between my ears. Anyone who can hit so precise a mark can easily pierce my throat or heart. Of course, the ptarmigan has vanished from the clearing along with my arrow.

By the time I reach the encampment, a large fire is blazing and several ptarmigan are being cleaned. I hold the offending arrow up to the fire light so that I can see how it differs from mine. I notice the arrowhead is dark grey whereas my arrowheads are light brown. I intend to look at the other men's arrowheads to see if I can find out whose are dark grey. This proves to be unnecessary for soon Zathrasook appears with a ptarmigan, *my* ptarmigan, which he gives to his mother to clean. Then he comes up to me, takes his arrow from my hand and gives me mine. He does this silently, never looking me in the face.

That night, we sleep sitting in a circle around the fire. I am positioned between Imamasduit and Tisewsut's wife and baby. Zathrasook sits opposite. As usual, he pays me no mind. In the distance, one wolf then another begins to howl. I think about the trick Zathrasook played on me. I ask myself why he wanted me to know it was *his* arrow that pinned me to the tree while he took my ptarmigan. As I sit listening to the wolves, the answer to this question comes to me. By tracking me as he did, Zathrasook was telling me that though the Osweet no longer shun me, as far as he's concerned, I am an enemy. He is reminding me that as a stranger and an outsider, I am at a disadvantage, and that he can kill me any time he likes.

9

We are now in our winter camp which is a day's walk past the second lake. This is a flat area with grassy clearings between the trees. We've camped here because of the caribou. When we first arrived seven days ago, the caribou were all around us, grazing in the clearings. Since then they have moved away. They're still close but have put some distance between themselves and us.

Our tent has been set up near a large round lake. I have learned that the Osweet call this tent a "mama-teek." The mamateek has been built in the same way as the other tents, with poles and birch-bark but it's much bigger, being large enough to hold us all. It has caribou skins on top of the bark to make it warmer inside. We all sleep with our toes toward the fire, bodies touching on either side. Now husbands and wives sleep together, and young children double up. There are eight sleeping places, most of them large enough to hold two or more. Three of us sleep alone: Abidith, Zathrasook and myself. I have been placed between Imamasduit and Abidith.

I am slowly learning to understand what my captors

say. I can't put exact meanings to words but I'm often able to sense what's being said. The Osweet don't talk at length. They speak slowly in a measured way which makes what they say easier to understand. I think they speak less than Greenlanders because they talk to one another in other ways. Now that the whole family lives inside one mamateek, I notice that some- one will know another's thoughts without a word being said. This is because movements and gestures speak instead. Just as a tilt of the head or a softening of the lips carry meaning, so too do the eyes. Now that I know the Osweet somewhat better, they also speak to me through these gestures and looks.

Only Abidith speaks inside my head. Usually this is at night before I sleep, or in the morning before I wake. Always when Abidith speaks to me, she's angry and scolding.

"You have much to learn, Wobee, before you can become one of us. You were captured by my people to take my brother's place. I don't think you can do that but Grandmother says it's possible you will become one of us some day. Since Grandmother holds the wisdom of our family, I will try to think as she does even though in this case, it goes against my will. It is not for you that I speak inside your head but for her."

Whenever Abidith enters my thoughts like this, I try to answer her back. I try to tell her that I would prefer Imamasduit speak to my thoughts herself, rather than someone who never lets me forget that I ran down her brother. I want to tell Abidith that in her place I too would be angry. If someone killed Magnus or Erling, I would go after him with an axe. I want to tell her that she might feel better if I had been killed. But I wasn't killed, I was taken captive, and there's nothing I can do to change those events. All of this I say to her inside my head. I have no way of knowing if she hears what I say. She never looks at me or gives any sign that she does. And I have no reason to think I have the power to enter her thoughts the way she can mine.

Now we are eating caribou, killing them one at a time, mainly strays the wolves have missed. We hear the wolves day and night. From them we know exactly where the caribou are. It's Bogodorasook's wish that before we have a caribou run, we should strengthen ourselves with meat. We set up racks for drying the caribou. We collect firewood. When this has been done, we prepare ourselves for the hunt and wait until the caribou position themselves where Bogodorasook wants. He says we must lure the caribou into our dreams to keep them close.

In Greenland men hunt deer which are much the same as caribou though slightly shorter in the legs. These deer are hunted on the island of Hreinsey which is a long way from our farm. My father's brother, who is a far better hunter than my father, was going to take me to Hreinsey this year. Probably he's there now.

Bogodorasook wants the caribou to follow a passageway we'll make beside the stream. This is the tail end of the river we've been following and which has now become a brook. It's narrow enough for the caribou to cross and escape into the woods. For this reason Bogodorasook bids us fell trees in such a way that they overlap each other to make a fence that will prevent the caribou from crossing the stream. Opposite the fence but on the same side of the stream, he has us stick poles into the ground in a line that follows the same turns as the fence. On top of the poles Bogodorasook ties tassels made from birch-bark. I don't know why he does this, but I assume the tassels serve a useful purpose. I have learned that the Osweet never do anything without good reason. When we're finished, there's a passageway between the fence and the line of poles all the way to the lake.

The morning of the hunt, we arm ourselves with bows and spears. There are seven of us altogether. Bogodorasook, Tisewsut and I take one of the canoes to the lake while Shawbawsut, Hathasut, Boasook and Zathrasook go into the woods and position themselves behind the caribou so that they can drive the animals through the passageway and into the lake where we will begin the slaughter.

We break the shore ice with our paddles, put the canoe into the water and paddle a short distance into the lake to wait. After a time, we hear yelling and shouting. I imagine the men behind the caribou jumping up and down in an effort to drive the animals through the passageway. Then we hear the caribou themselves, snorting and huffing. They are coming along the passageway, eight or nine caribou pounding over the snow toward the lake. At the water's edge, the caribou stop. In the distance Shawbawsut shouts that the main herd is coming this way. The caribou on the shore of the lake plunge into the water and begin swimming to the opposite shore. With skilful paddling, Bogodorasook steers the canoe to intercept the swimming caribou. He's already told me that the way to hunt caribou from a boat is to plunge my spear into an animal's neck and hold its head under until it drowns.

Tisewsut is already doing this. He plunges the spear deep, forcing the animal's head underwater. As soon as the caribou ceases to struggle, Tisewsut removes the spear.

A second caribou swims close by. Bogodorasook positions the canoe so that I can spear it, which I do. The spearing itself isn't difficult but it requires all my strength to keep the animal's head underwater.

Tisewsut and I kill another caribou before the other hunters reach the shore. I have been far too occupied to count the number of caribou which have gained the opposite shore but I know most of them have escaped. Zathrasook and Shawbawsut now have the other canoe in the water. They are trying to head off the caribou we miss. Hathasut and Boasook remain on shore to prevent the animals from retreating along the passageway. They use their bows as well as spears to bring down animals close to shore. Bogodorasook tells us to begin towing the carcasses ashore where we will remove the antlers and feet. The caribou float on the water which makes towing them easy work. Soon the shore water seethes with blood.

While we are moving carcasses ashore, I look up and see a large stag enter the lake. Without any forethought, I run after the stag and plunge my spear into his neck. Bogodorasook is saying something to me but I can't make out what it is above the animal's loud snort. With no thought of the consequences, I leap onto the animal's back, stretch forward and push its head under. The stag rears up and plunges toward deeper water. I hold on and rock his antlers back and forth while the stag swims toward the other side of the lake. The caribou twists its body and I'm thrown off. Before I can swim free, I feel myself being pushed below the surface of the lake by the weight of the caribou. A hoof pounds my head and I lose sight of everything, the water, the caribou, the sky.

When my eyes open, I am near the bottom of the lake. I can see nothing except the huge dark body far above me on top of the water. My chest burns for want of air. I try to hold my breath. Water seeps into my nose and mouth. I choke and gasp. I know I have to get to the surface of the water but I don't have the strength to lift myself up.

Now a strange thing happens. My mind begins to separate itself from my body. It seems to be floating up and up, out of the lake, while my body is sinking lower and lower. My mind has reached the surface of the lake. It goes higher and higher, into the air. Now I am looking down on myself. Below me in the murky water is the body of a young man drowning in the lake.

TWO

Two

10

We are inside our mamateek watching Grandmother and Grandfather perform. Both of them are draped in caribou hides and wear antlers on their heads so that we will forget they are people and imagine them as animals instead.

There are two caribou: a female and a male. They have flat antlers, heavy grey fur, short ears and tails. The larger of the two puts his nose to the female's and licks her nose, then her flank. For a long time the caribou stand together licking and nuzzling each other. Then they mate. When the mating is finished, they put their heads to the ground and eat. They pull the grass into their mouths and tug it loose. Every so often, the caribou lift their heads, though not at the same time, to look around and sniff the air. Eventually they stop eating and begin to walk, the female leading, the male following. They walk and walk, crossing streams and lakes. The male still follows the female, though somewhat behind. The trail the caribou are using is between the rising and the setting sun. After they have journeyed long enough, they put their heads down again in a clearing and graze.

The caribou have been alert and watchful, but unafraid. Now, sensing danger, the male lifts his head and snorts. The female lifts her head and paws the ground. Both of them look for the hunters they know are there but can't see. The eyes of the caribou become wild and crazed. They know by the smell that their lives are at risk. Their heads jerk up. They begin first to trot, then to run. They run along a narrow passageway, a pile of brushwood on one side, a row of tasselled poles on the other. The tassels frighten them. They run, bumping into and colliding with each other until they come to a lake. Here they hesitate, unable to go back because of the caribou coming behind, unwilling to plunge into the freezing water where hunters wait in boats. Snorting and puffing they plunge into the water and begin to swim. They don't get far before the male and then the female are speared in the neck. They roll sideways in the water and kick their legs. Screams of terror pierce the air. The caribou beat the water with their hooves. Their antlers bob and twist then sink. Gradually their struggle weakens to nothing more than fitful trembles and jerks. Finally it stops altogether. The caribou corpses float on the lake.

The mime is finished. Grandmother and Grand-father shed their caribou skins and antlers and join the rest of us on the ground. Now comes the part of the evening I like best. The dance. My mother rises to her feet. Though she has lived more than thirty years and is somewhat thickened by child-bearing, she is still graceful and supple. Her long hair falls over her shoulders. Her feet and arms are bare. She's wearing her dancing dress which is made of softened caribou skin that hangs in a straight line from above her chest to her knees. The top and bottom of the dress are fringed. My mother lifts her arms up and moves first to one side then the other. As she moves, the rest of us begin to chant and hum. Anticipating the music, my mother matches her movements to the voices of the rhythm. Holding her arms high, she sways to the accompaniment and drops her head so that her hair moves in a wide liquid circle. She bends forward, circling from the waist. The circle grows larger and spreads. Then the music changes and our chanting becomes high and shrill. My mother stands upright and moves in thrusts and jerks. Her body becomes a knife cutting the air, thrusting and jabbing here then there. Her hair tosses back and forth.

Tisewsut takes out a bird-bone whistle and begins to play. The chanting and humming stops. My mother continues to dance, not only to the whistle's tune but also to the music inside her head. Faster and faster she dances, jerking her arms and legs in a frenzy, hair flying every which way. Sweat glistens on her shoulders and arms. Her lips open: she is panting hard. Her feet pound the floor. The whistle stops but she keeps on dancing, her eyes shining, focused not on us but the invisible others who are always there. She is no longer my mother but Thoowidith the dancer. She dances until finally her knees bend and fold. Then she drops, kneeling to the floor.

We watch and wait for Thoowidith to get to her feet and take her place as mother, grandmother, wife. We know that we must not spoil it by moving or speaking until the dancer has gotten up and again become one of us.

Grandmother and Grandfather get to their feet and take a pot from beside the fire where it has been set to warm. Holding it between them, they dip a stick into the mixture of grease and marrow inside and give each of us a taste. The marrow is made from caribou bones that have been boiled and mashed. By eating the marrow, we are showing our respect for the spirit of the caribou so that as long as time lasts, the spirit will allow us to follow the movements of the animal herds. When all of us have eaten the marrow, Grandmother and Grandfather go to the fire where the venison of the large stag has been roasted. While Grandfather cuts the meat, Grandmother carries it to us, placing a small slice on each of our tongues. Only when everyone, including the smallest child among us, has been served, does the ceremony of the caribou end and we begin to talk.

I cannot take my eyes from my mother. Although she's now sitting beside my father, doing something as ordinary as chewing meat, I can't quite believe she's my mother. While she was dancing, my mother, Thoowidith, was transformed into someone else, someone with special powers, someone who saw beyond where we are now. There was a reddish light around her that came from another place. That was when I knew my mother was dancing with our ancestors, that she was dancing for our invisible dead, including my brother, and in so doing, joined them to us.

I have never seen the invisible others. Grandmother has assured me that this will eventually happen, that I will come to know our ancestors one day. Grandmother said that when they were ready, our Osweet ancestors would speak to me. My mother has told me that I must wait for them to come to me. I know that unless and until this happens, I will never become a dancer like my mother.

We Osweet have only one dancer. It is always a woman. Whoever replaces my mother one day will be chosen by our ancestors. It might be my sister, Dysee, who has a young daughter and is far gone with child. It might be Zathrasook's married sister, Adensit, who's also the mother of daughters. Or it might be Zathrasook's younger sister, Merooish.

More than anything else, more than becoming a wife and mother, I want to be chosen as the one to dance. For me the dancer is the one among us who feels the most joy. Grandmother says that what people most need to feel is contentment and calm. She says I must learn to set aside anger if I am to find peace. I am sure this is true. Even so, whenever I watch the caribou dance, I know my mother is feeling something besides contentment and calm. I see it in her eyes, in the way she moves. I can't describe what she feels. I can't give it any name except joy, but I think it's the same thing birds feel when they fly, or whales when they leap out of the sea.

I watch Grandmother approach Wobee. When he reaches for the meat, she gently guides his hand away. Wobee doesn't know the first piece must come from Grandmother's hand for she has the spirit of the caribou inside her tonight. The stag we are eating is the one Wobee brought down. It's our custom when feasting to feed everyone with the largest animal killed.

By the time the men dragged Wobee from the lake and brought him to the fire, he was stiff with cold and unable to speak. His clothes were so wet and muddy, he had to be stripped. He was laid on furs beside the fire while Grandmother and I rubbed his limbs. I did not want to touch him but Grandmother insisted I do. How strange it was to see the whiteness of his body which felt soft and slippery to the touch, like the underbelly of a fish. How odd it felt to be rubbing that skin. Grandmother and I rubbed until Wobee's body shivered and warmed and he opened his eyes. When Wobee saw us bending over him, he rolled onto his belly to hide his private parts. Grandmother covered him with a robe and he remained under it while his clothes dried beside the fire.

Wobee nearly drowned. A story will be made of this after our feast is over and the tale-telling begins.

Then I will find out how Wobee's near drowning came about. I choose a piece of meat Grandfather has sliced and put into a birch-bark container so that each of us can help ourselves. How good it is for us to be able to eat until we are full.

Such abundance can never be taken for granted. Some winters—there have been two in my lifetime— meat is scarce and we go without food until our bellies shrink and shrivel inside. But when our hunters make a large kill, we can eat as much as we want. There were six caribou killed today. The herd is close and large which means we will have enough meat to carry us through the Winter.

Some years the caribou spirit is displeased and hides the caribou so they are hard to find. Last year only three caribou were seen in the woods near our camp and we often went to bed hungry. As a result, no children were conceived at that time. Later on Dysee conceived, after some beaver were killed, but she was the only woman among us who did.

After we have finished eating, the tale-telling begins. Grandfather says that the tale-telling is part of the feast, that we are as hungry for stories as we are for meat. He says we need such food if we are to keep our heads alive. It's possible, he says, to starve the head, for the head eats stories, instead of meat. If the head goes without eating, Grandfather says, it too will shrivel and die.

Grandmother will tell the first tale. Every feast time

she tells us the story of where we come from. This story may or may not be true. We know this, but it doesn't matter. What matters is that the story is there for each of us to believe or disbelieve as we choose and in so choosing discover our own truth. As Grandmother has said many times, the knowledge of our making is unknown to us for it comes from inside the head of the Creator which is larger than any of ours. That is why Grandmother makes up stories to explain how our coming-to-be-here might have been.

Grandmother begins with the story of how the Creator roamed the land with his bow and arrows, hunting and sleeping at will. He went on in this way, stopping whenever and wherever he chose. He journeyed far and wide, sometimes on foot, sometimes by canoe. Eventually he grew weary of travelling alone and longed for the company of others. He didn't know who these others might be since he had never known anyone except himself. One day when he was sitting beside the fire outside his summer tent, he took the arrows from his sheath and stuck them into the ground one by one. As he did this, the arrows turned into men and women. The Creator put so many arrows into the ground that soon there was a crowd of people walking about. Unused to the company of others, the Creator picked them up and turned them back into arrows. The Creator fitted the arrows into a bow and shot them far away so that the people would be spread about. Some of the people fell across the wide water to the West; some fell beside the sea, others in the woods. That is why there are Owasposhno-un, Washawet and Osweet, for not everyone is born in the same place.

After Grandmother finishes the story, it's time for the hunting tales to be told. These tales begin with the hunts of long ago before our people built fences to trap the caribou. In those days, the winters weren't so cold and food was easier to find. There weren't as many red people then either. In those days the caribou were killed in twos and threes. There was no need to store food against the day when it would be scarce.

Now all that is changed. The caribou spirit doesn't allow the animals to wander freely on their own but herds them together so they must be hunted in groups. That is why our hunters must build fences and work together.

The men begin telling stories of different hunts they've been on over the years. These tales are about the unexpected, when either the caribou or the hunter offers some surprise. They are about the challenge of the hunt when a man must match his skill with the caribou's. Although it doesn't happen often, a hunter never forgets that the caribou can overpower him, that if he isn't quick-headed or fast-footed enough, his life will be forfeited, instead of the caribou's. The men tell their stories in the order they occurred, beginning with the oldest tales and ending with Grandfather telling the story of how Wobee killed the largest stag.

"Wobee's on the lake shore when a large stag enters the water. Wobee goes after him and thrusts his spear into the stag's neck and tries to hold him down. But the stag is strong and keeps his head above the lake. Wobee leaps onto the stag's back and, leaning forward, holds onto his antlers, trying to twist the head underwater. The stag is powerful and swims toward the far side of the lake. Wobee is strong too and holds on. Suddenly the stag rears up and twists, throwing Wobee off, pounding him with his hoof. Wobee sinks like a stone. But the stag is also in trouble for his neck wound is bleeding bad. He begins to die and we leave him to do this, knowing he will never reach shore alive. Zathrasook and Shawbawsut search the water for Wobee. They paddle round and round but there's no sign of him anywhere. Then they see him near the bottom. Zathrasook dives down and pulls Wobee into the canoe. Shawbawsut pushes Wobee on the chest until he coughs out water and begins to breathe. Shawbawsut takes off his robe and wraps it around Wobee before he and Tisewsut bring Wobee to the fire and Zathrasook and I tow the stag ashore."

The storytelling makes us sleepy. Content with the warmth and the food, we crawl to our sleeping places. After I'm settled beneath the covers, I think about the story of Wobee's near drowning. I was watching Zathrasook when Grandfather was telling the tale. I saw Zathrasook's disappointment that the caribou spirit had given the largest stag to Wobee, instead of himself. I know we cannot question what the caribou spirit does, but to me it seems unfair that this white stranger should earn what is rightfully ours, for it cannot mean the same to him as it does to us. If Zathrasook had been the one to kill the largest stag, he would have earned the right to wear our totem, which Wobee cannot do. How strange that it was Zathrasook who pulled Wobee from the lake. Perhaps he thought Wobee was a corpse by then. If he had known Wobee was alive, would he have rescued him? Is his hatred of Wobee still so strong he wishes him dead? Or has it softened a little like mine? I do not like Wobee, but I am learning not to hate him. Grandmother has told me that my hatred of Wobee will not harm him as much as it will harm myself.

The next day, our hunters go out again and return with four caribou. Now the high branches of trees outside our mamateek are decorated with antlers and the frozen meat of the caribou. This time Zathrasook spears a large stag but it isn't as large as Wobee's, which means he still cannot wear our totem. For many days we women are kept busy scraping the hides, making soups and stews, cleaning the sinews and entrails for later use.

The men cut antlers into small pieces for whittling amulets and tools. They cut strips of skin for snowshoe webbing. Tisewsut and Boasook go into the forest and cut saplings which they bend into loops and lash to crossbeams to make snowshoes. Though there's snow on the ground, the weather is mild enough for the men to work outside around the fire.

As usual we women work around the fire inside. Whenever I pass the men outside, I see Wobee carving something from a piece of wood. I don't go close enough to find out what it is, but I am curious about what it could be. Usually we women work in silence but this silence is sometimes broken with talk about men. We talk about the marriages that will take place at next summer's gathering, who will marry who, where they will live. Usually the wife lives with her husband's family. But these last years it hasn't always been so. Though Tisewsut is Owasposhno-un and Hathasut is Washawet, both men live with us. This is because there is a shortage of men among us. Grandmother bore two children, my father and and his sister Woasut. My mother bore two daughters and a son Awadasut; Woasut also bore two daughters and a son Zathrasook. The children of these daughters have both been girls. This has upset the balance of men and women in our family. Without young men to marry off, we are at a disadvantage with the Owasposhno-un and the Washawet when it comes to making marriage arrangements and trading goods.

This was the main reason Wobee was captured. If he survives, he will eventually be used, instead of my brother, to marry into the Owasposhno-un or the Washawet and in that way strengthen our trading position. Whatever we women think inside our heads about Wobee doesn't matter. What matters is the survival of our people. This is what Grandmother and Grandfather say to us and what they themselves believe to be true.

"It may be that the Owasposhno-un or the Washawet won't want a stranger marrying one of them," Woasut says. Of all the women, including myself, she most resents Wobee's presence among us, especially since her son, Zathrasook, was denied the largest stag.

"He won't be a stranger," Grandmother says, "once he learns our ways."

"He will always be a stranger," Woasut insists.

"Am I a stranger to you?" Grandmother smiles.

Woasut shakes her head no.

"Yet I was Owasposhno-un a long time ago, before I became Osweet."

"But the Osweet and Owasposhno-un are the same."

"We didn't spring from the same arrow," says Grandmother. "The Creator aimed his arrows so that we fell in different places. It may be that Wobee springs from an arrow that was carried further away."

"It may be that Wobee didn't spring from an arrow at all," Woasut says.

"In two more years Abidith will marry an Owasposhno-un or a Washawet," my mother says, to change the conversation. "Who do you think it will be?" She rubs her hand against my cheek, more to tease I think than to soothe, for she knows I am reluctant to think about the decision before the summer gathering.

My husband will either be Watsut of the Owasposhno-un, or Koorsook of the Washawet; they are the only men among our people who are neither too old nor too young for me. I am not ready to choose between the two. When I saw them a year and a half ago, they were boys. Of the two, I liked Watsut better because he was kind and made me laugh. But he may be different now. For this reason, I try not to prefer him to Koorsook; or to think of either one very much. But this doesn't stop the other women from discussing what kind of husband they think Watsut and Koorsook will make.

Fortunately, the conversation turns to Dysee's baby. My sister rubs her belly which is huge; the baby will be born soon.

"It's a boy, I'm sure of it," Dysee says. "He kicks and elbows me so much he is already pretending to be on the hunt."

"Even so, we won't make his birth clothes yet," my mother says.

Because babies sometimes die at birth, it's our custom to make the birth clothes only after the baby has emerged alive and strong.

Two days after the second caribou hunt, Dysee wakens

from sleep with a gasp. It's the middle of the afternoon and she's been having a nap. The men are outside; we women inside working in silence, so as not to waken Dysee. Dysee gasps again.

"Help me up," she says.

I find her boots and put them on her feet. Then I help her stand. Our mother wraps a caribou skin around Dysee and leads her outside. For the next while, Dysee walks about the enclosure. Until the pains come stronger and closer together, she will stay on her feet and continue to walk.

The men gather their weapons and go off to the woods, leaving the camp to the women. Today the men are going after a fox whose thick fur will be used for the baby's bed.

We take turns walking on either side of Dysee, our arms around her shoulders. One of us carries a stout stick. When a pain seizes Dysee's back, she grabs the stick and squeezes hard until the pain subsides, then she continues walking. Both fires are kept burning. Inside the mamateek we prepare the birth place and line it with moss. We take a pole, newly cut and trimmed, and pound it into the ground until it stands upright. We set a stone knife by the fire and heat water by dropping hot rocks into a container of water. The nearby stream is frozen over, but the ice is easily broken which makes fetching water an easy chore.

By nightfall, the pains are coming in rapid succession and Dysee is led into the mamateek. She holds onto the pole and squats above the birth place. By then the men have returned from the woods and sit around the fire outside, skinning a fox they have killed. I know they hear the cries and moans coming from inside the mamateek but they give no indication they themselves are distressed. Like us, the men have heard the cries of childbirth before and know they will pass.

Woasut and Adensit leave us, taking the younger children with them. The children find their sleeping places by the fire outside. Inside we continue our vigil.

Halfway through the night, there's a long anguished groan. This is followed by a squall that reminds me of a seal pup's mewl. The squall is faint at first but soon grows into a lusty yell. Now we are shouting and whooping with laughter.

Grandmother goes outside and tells the others that Dysee has given birth to a son.

"A big strong boy with a wide chest and a large head."

Dysee lies on the mossy birth place. I sit beside her and wipe the sweat from her brow. Our mother pushes Dysee's swollen belly until the afterbirth eases out. Imamasduit has cut the baby's birth cord and he now lies in the crook of Dysee's arm. He's bluish red with the wrinkled face of an old man and a covering of wet black hair on his head.

"How beautiful he is," my sister murmurs.

Grandmother returns and takes the baby close to the fire. She puts him on a bed of moss and washes him clean. Then she packs him with moss and bundles him in deerskin. All the while, the child cries and Grandmother talks softly to him.

"A noisy one we have here," she says. "He has a lot to say for himself."

She returns the baby to Dysee.

Now the others come inside and gather round. Such is the joy and happiness of our people that no one wants to be outside. None of us sleeps in our accustomed places. We arrange ourselves in piles and heaps around Dysee and the baby and stay there throughout the night.

The next day, Grandmother sews the baby's clothes from deerskin she has softened by chewing. My mother lines a bed of birch-bark with fox fur. I set a pot of ptarmigan and water to stew; together Adensit and I put a caribou roast on the spit. Then we mix dried berries, caribou fat and dried birds' eggs crushed into powder and shape them into cakes.

We sweep the mamateek clean and put fresh spruce boughs in the sleeping hollows. When all this has been done, everyone gathers inside to watch my mother give the birth dance. My mother has tucked a skin beneath her dancing dress to make herself look swollen with child. As she dances, she makes large circles in the air with her arms. Then she adds another skin beneath her dress and makes more circles. She continues doing this, never breaking the rhythm until her belly is huge. Now she begins to jerk and thrust, arching her back, tilting her head. She moans and cries. Her hair flies about. The dance quickens and her feet pound the floor. She squats and the roll of skins drops to the floor. She sweeps them up and bundles them to her, crooning and singing. Then she dances around the room, holding out the skin baby for everyone to see and touch. At last she places the bundle at Dysee's feet.

Now the feasting begins. Dysee is served first. Imamasduit tells her to eat as much as she pleases. Everyone is hungry, especially for the stew and cakes, but no one eats until my sister has had her fill.

When the feasting is over, Wobee gets up and places something on top of the baby's chest. It's the piece of wood I saw him carving earlier. It's a flat object of some kind with a handle attached. I don't know what it is. I see Dysee pick it up and turn it over. She doesn't know what it is either. Dysee is careful not to look at Wobee so he won't see the question in her eyes. But he sees it anyway. He takes the carving and pretends to scoop food from the stew pot and put it into his mouth. Then he returns the carving to the baby. He has made an eating tool for my sister's son. Surely Wobee has noticed that we don't eat with tools. Quickly I snatch the tool away. It is bad to give the baby something he has no use for. I wrap the tool in a piece of skin and tuck it behind the firewood, near the door. Now that we've been fortunate to have a boy child, I won't risk having anything close by that might cause him harm. I see Grandmother speaking to Wobee. She's telling him that until he's been strengthened by a name, the baby must be protected from the unknown. Later, after he's been named and ochred at the summer gathering, the eating tool can be given to him and he can do with it what he likes. I know from the way he holds his head that Wobee is disappointed to have the tool he made put away, but he must learn to follow our ways and leave his behind.

That night while we are sleeping the wind becomes strong and fierce. It sweeps over the clearing, blowing snow everywhere. The storm continues all the next day and night. It grows cold. On the third morning, when the wind dies and we look outside, we see that drifting snow has filled in the clearing. A rush of bitter cold sweeps inside. The men put on their robes and snowshoes and go outside to clear pathways and cut firewood. They bring in frozen caribou meat for us to cook. From now on, each day is much like the next. The men clear snow and snowshoe into the forest to look for small game. We women cook and sew. We don't go far from the mamateek, not even to the stream which is now frozen solid. Instead we drink melted snow. Late afternoons, after we have eaten and before it grows dark, we tell stories. Grandmother asks Wobee if he has any stories. He replies that his people, the Greenlanders, have stories so old that they were told them by the Icelanders who in turn were told them by the Norwegians, who came from a country very far from here. Grandmother urges Wobee to tell us a story and eventually he does. It is a story full of strange creatures and words, and reminds me again how different Wobee is from us.

"In the beginning there was no earth, only a vast emptiness called Ginnungagap with the land of fire in the South and the land of cold in the North. Below Ginnungagap was the well of life where there was nothing but mist and ice. Out of this freezing drizzle came Ymir, father of the frost giants and Audumla, the cow that fed Ymir milk. When Audumla licked the ice, the god Buri came out and mated with Bestla. They had three sons of whom Odin was the greatest. Odin and his brothers killed Ymir and threw his body into the void of Ginnungagap. From his body came the world. His ice blood became the sea and his flesh the land. Mountains were made from his shoulders and knees. Odin took sparks from the land of fire and made the stars. He also made the sun and moon. He made trees and grass from Ymir's hair and clouds from his breath. Odin made the first man and woman from trees and set them in a place called Middle Earth. Giants and trolls also lived in Middle Earth. Dwarves also lived there, in caves.

"It was dwarves who made rings and jewelled swords for kings. In the centre of the earth was the Tree in which the gods lived. Odin sat at the top, sometimes disguised as an eagle. At other times a raven sat on each of Odin's shoulders and wolves lay at his feet. A serpent was coiled around the base of the Tree, gnawing at its roots. Beneath the Tree near a spring lived the three sisters weaving the fate of other folk. Thor and the other gods used to meet here every day to settle disputes."

Much of Wobee's story is difficult for us to understand. It is hard for us to make pictures from his words. We are full of questions.

"What is a cow and how did she feed Ymir?"

"What are dwarves and trolls?"

"What is a serpent?"

"Can the Tree be seen from here?"

"What were sisters doing beneath the Tree?"

Wobee explains that a cow is an animal somewhat like a caribou that lives in fields and gives people milk.

"What is milk?"

"White water."

"That explains the colour of your skin."

"How does milk come out of a cow?"

He tells how the milk is squeezed into a large container then poured into smaller cups.

"Isn't the cow spirit offended by taking food intended for its young?"

"There is no cow spirit."

Zathrasook breaks in. "See how he mocks us."

"I don't mock you."

Zathrasook persists.

"We should never tell our tales in front of him."

"We aren't telling our tales," Imamasduit reminds

him. "At my request we are listening to his. Tell us about dwarves, trolls and serpents."

Wobee explains that dwarves and trolls are small, ugly folk who live in underground places, for they prefer the dark to the light. He says dwarves make beautiful objects which they give to kings. He tells us serpents are snakes.

"Snakes. What are snakes?"

"Giant worms with huge, ugly mouths. They coil themselves around you and squeeze you to death. Thor tried to kill a sea serpent once."

A shudder of revulsion passes through us. My mother asks Wobee why the three sisters lived beneath the Tree.

"They are making cloth. In Greenland we have animals called sheep whose wool coverings can be woven into cloth which we use to dress ourselves. At the same time the sisters are weaving the cloth, they are also making our future. They know before we do what will happen to us."

This to me is the strangest thing of all, that anyone should know what will happen to someone else ahead of time.

"I don't understand your gods," Bogodorasook says. "Which one is your Creator?"

"In the beginning Ymir was the Creator."

"But he was killed by another man. What was his name?"

"Odin."

"Why would Odin kill the Creator?"

"I don't know," Wobee says. "I've never thought to ask."

"It seems strange for a god to kill the being who created himself, the Earth and its people," Bogodora-sook says quietly. "I couldn't honour a god like that."

"It's just a story," Wobee says. "We have other stories, not about gods but about our leaders."

"Tell us one."

Wobee is reluctant to do this, but finally, with Grandfather's urging, he tells us this story:

"King Havadan was King of Norway. His wife Queen Ragnhild was a woman who had mighty dreams. Once she dreamed a huge tree bled over Norway. King Havadan couldn't dream at all unless he slept with the pigs, which he did."

Wobee explains pigs are fat animals that lie in the mud, and we all laugh, even Zathrasook, picturing a man sleeping with animals in the mud.

"The King dreamed locks of many coloured hair grew out of his head and spread everywhere. Wise folk interpreted the King and Queen's dreams as foretelling Harald's birth, for soon after the dreaming, Harald was born. Later when Harald grew into a man, King Havadan's sled went through rotten ice and he drowned. Harald became King in his father's stead. King Havadan had been so well loved that his corpse was cut into four pieces and buried in various places in Norway where they became known as Havadan's howes."

Tisewsut asks about kings and queens.

"Kings are leaders of the land and are married to queens. They are rich and have more goods than other folk," Wobee says. Then he asks, "Do you have such leaders over here?"

For a long while no one replies. Then Bogodora-sook says, "Our leaders have no more, no less than other people. It is better that way."

"But who is the leader of the whole land?"

"The Creator."

"Is he a god?"

"He is the Creator."

He tells him that the King of Norway burns people out of their beds unless they swear allegiance to the Christian god who is also the Creator.

Bogodorasook smiles at this. "A King and a Creator. Now that is asking for trouble. Our people have no such leaders but we sleep peacefully at night."

Because daylight is short, night begins early. When darkness falls we no longer tell stories but drift into silence that soon becomes sleep. Sometimes we are awakened by the hoot of an owl or the howl of wolves, but not often. There aren't many owls in these woods and the wolves have moved off with the cari-bou herd. While we sleep we dream, dreaming much of the Winter away. Wobee also dreams. I know this because I sometimes see his dreams.

I have listened closely to what Grandmother has said about dreams. She has said there is so much we do not know about ourselves that appears in dreams. She says the origin of dreams is to be found in another time and place. She says dreams picture our longings. It is these dream pictures, she says, that shape our lives. It is the same for everyone she says. Sometimes we live inside one another's dreams. I know this to be true because when I see Wobee's dreams they are as real and frightening to me as if they were happening to myself.

In my dream it's night-time. The air over the meadow is clear and cold. There's a white moon in the sky. The moon is the centre of my belly, the centre of my womb. My womb is full of water. In the water is a baby, as rounded and perfect as an unhatched egg. The egg bobs on the water. It rocks back and forth with the tide. The tide brings in shells and flowers, it brings in fish. The fish are silvery and leap in the waves.

The moon is a round O in the face of night. Its breath is the frost whitening the landscape, making everything shine. It breathes on the stag standing in the meadow, and on me astride his back. The stag's eyes glitter in the moonlight. I touch his flank. The stag runs across the meadow. He runs fast, faster, and then he flies. He rises to the sky, with me on his back.

"Take me home," I whisper, thinking of distant

mountains gleaming in moonlight, dreaming in the darkness that is Winter there.

The stag flies above the forest. I don't look down. I will fall into a pit of spears if I look down.

The moon is a stone. It is a perfect stone the Creator has made. There are some stones that look white in the moonlight, but when I hold one in the palm of my hand, they lose their whiteness and become brown or grey. The Creator's stone is pure white, as white as the moon. When we are given a pure white stone, it is an omen of hope made by the Creator himself.

The moon is Odin's eye. Odin sits far from me on his throne above Heaven and Earth. On each shoulder is a raven, at his feet two wolves. Odin's eye glitters coldly as it watches my struggle to live in this red world. Odin speaks with his eye. He tells me it is all for nothing, this struggle, for the sisters sitting at their looms beneath the Tree have stopped weaving my fate, and Thor is too busy to look for me. I see a serpent gnawing at the roots of the Tree. Strange fruits tumble down and are eaten by a cow. Odin turns into an eagle and flies away.

I dance and the moon becomes the eye of a whale leaping and splashing in a silver sea. Water rises into spray and foam. The whale stands on its tail and begins to sing. It sings of fish and birds, of walrus and seals, of caribou and bears, of seaweed and kelp, of beaches and rocks. It sings of snow and ice, of the cold clear air of northern lands.

I dance and dance. The whale sings of the earth's turning, of its changing from cold to warmth. The whale sings of melting rivers and streams, of lakes and ponds, of ice breaking from land and plunging into the sea. It sings of the migrations of birds and fish. The whale sings until his eye turns a fiery red. Then he dives deep into the sea and is gone.

The sun is a fire ring in the sky. I have ridden all night and am shivering with sweat despite the cold. I leap from the stag and stand beneath the fire willing the heat to make me dry. As I turn my face up to the sky, I see benches and stools whirl into the fire. Sparks leap up and vanish as daytime stars. Clouds rise from mountains and shape themselves into a ship that is slowly licked into nothingness by the sun's hungry tongues. As I watch, three looms fall into the flames and the weavers' cloth burns. The Tree crashes down and catches fire. At last, when the Tree is consumed, the fire becomes a glowing ring that sinks lower and lower in the sky. It disappears and I am left shivering in the dark, groping for something to grab hold of, a leaf or a twig.

The sun rises on another day. It is the Creator's head appearing at the place where the sea meets the sky. The Creator wades ashore. He plucks a tree from the forest and makes himself a bow. Then he makes arrows with heads that glow with fire. One by one, the Creator fits the flaming arrows to his bow and pointing it upward, shoots. When the arrows fall to the ground, they become Grandmother and Grandfather. More arrows fall to the ground, becoming other people who run about in the sun. People are content, for they do not suffer for want of food. They wade into the sea and harvest lobsters and clams. They walk into the woods and find caribou and bear waiting there. They stroll across green meadows, plucking whatever berries they choose to eat. The bushes are laden with red and purple fruit. The abundance of the Creator is so great that hunger doesn't exist.

Before the day is finished, the Creator takes some earth from his head and forms a giant ball. The ball flames around its edge but doesn't burn the Creator's hands. The Creator flings the ball against a rocky cliff and the cliff becomes red. Then the Creator walks back into the sea. The water comes up to his knees, his waist, his shoulders. The Creator disappears beyond the sea. But he has left his head behind. The head shines on the water, making a trail of red, showing us the path he followed when he came out of the sea.

Three

11

The spoon I gave the baby was very like the spoon I had as a small child. The Osweet don't have spoons, and I thought once I showed them how one was used, it would be welcome. Dysee and Abidith mistrusted my intention which was to please. Like the others, I felt pleasure at the birth of the baby, and wanted to provide something that would honour his being. I wanted to share the joy.

I can't remember there being such joyfulness about a birth among my own people in Greenland though I suppose the joy was there. I always took the presence of my younger brothers for granted. I never thought their births remarkable in any way: one day there was a baby beside the hearth in a place that had been empty before. I had been curious about the new baby but no more than that.

With the birth of Dysee's baby I felt differently. I felt the wonder of new life being born. I saw the happiness a new child can bring. I saw how it transformed the Osweet, how it drew them more closely together, how pleased they were with the mother and her child. I think my parents must have been closely drawn together when my sister and brothers were born, but I had been too young to notice. No doubt I had other things on my mind.

I have never been one to show my feelings. Many Greenlanders regard it as a sign of weakness to reveal their gentler side. This may be why I took such pleasure in carving the spoon, for I put my feelings into it. I took the sadness I felt about Awadasut's death which came to me first in a dream, and carved it on the spoon handle in the shape of a weeping man. Then I carved a baby sitting on the shoulders of the man. I did this instinctively, not understanding why I designed it so until later on. The designs are crude for I am not yet skilled with rock tools. When it was complete, I realized my carving was an attempt to connect birth and death, joy and sadness. The spoon has not been used. Soon after I gave it to the baby, Abidith hid it away as if it was a bad luck omen and I haven't seen it since.

Despite this, I don't regret making the spoon, for I learned something about myself while I was carving it. Before coming to Leifsbudir I had carved only bone and once a piece of walrus ivory from which I made my mother a needle case. Even with iron tools, I found the carving tedious and unrewarding. Bone and ivory were too difficult for my skills. Until lately, I had never carved wood. Because of the scarcity of wood in Greenland, there was none to spare for carving. And there were always chores to do. Here there is such an abundance of wood and time that I find I enjoy carving. It's painstaking work. Stone knives are sharper than iron but must be frequently repointed. But carving helps me understand myself. I have discovered that it feels good to know I can turn understanding into something firm and solid in my hands. The knowledge takes away my loneliness and allows me to forget my circumstances. Fortunately, there's more daylight here which means if it isn't stormy, I can sit outside with the other men, working close by the fire. This wouldn't be possible in Greenland, for the sun never appears there in Winter and we Greenlanders are forced to spend most of our time indoors, where oil lamps provide meager light and heat.

Running the length of my calendar stick are two branches intertwined. The straighter of the branches represents my desire to go home; the other shows how I feel about my captors. This branch twists and knots itself in several places showing how tangled my feelings for these people are. At Imamasduit's and Bogodorasook's urging, most of the Osweet are now kind and helpful to me and I like them for it. When the time comes, this liking will make it more difficult for me to escape. After I finish the carving, I rub the stick with caribou grease to make it shiny and smooth. Six months have been notched into my stick. Each day when I make a new groove, I remind myself of my resolve, which is that in another six months, I will make my way back to Leifsbudir.

During these winter months, Abidith and I have become companions, or so I think. It may be she does not regard me as a companion and pretends friendliness in order to keep watch on me. For Abidith has the power to penetrate my thoughts, especially my dreams. I have no proof of this, but at night I can sometimes feel her presence inside my head. It's as if I am in a clearing and she is in the woods watching me. Early in my captivity, when I first felt her presence in this way, she was angry and scolding. Now her presence, while not gentle, is more restrained, as if she was waiting for me to do or say something rash. I have tried many times to strengthen my thoughts so that they can enter hers, but try as I may, I remain outside, and she is impenetrable to me. This puts me at a disadvantage, for it means she can enter my secret places whereas I cannot enter hers. I feel as helpless and naked as I did when I realized she and Imamasduit were rubbing my body after my near drowning, in an effort to make me warm.

One night I have this dream: Abidith and I are standing on a beach to the West. Beside us are bundles of food and clothing. We are saying goodbye to Imamasduit and the others. We load our goods into a pram. This is a boat I have built of sprucewood. Abidith and I get into the pram and row away, waving at the Osweet along the shore. Abidith is now my wife and I am taking her to meet my family in Greenland. We do not stay in Greenland but sail southward, looking for a land that is perpetually warm.

In the morning when I awaken, I am shy about looking at Abidith who is already by the fire, her back to me. Does she know she was inside my dream? She does not turn and look at me, but continues to feed the fire so I cannot tell if she knows my dream. I will never know. I feel a fluttering inside my chest. It's as if a small bird is caged there. Not only has my body been captured, but my thoughts as well. How can I escape from the Osweet if I can't hide anything from Abidith? When the time comes to make my plans, she will know what they are before I can get away.

12

The last winter storm sweeps through our camp. Snow drifts against the mamateek and except for a path from the entryway, we leave the snow where it is, for the drift provides us with extra warmth. We seldom need go far since we cut a large supply of firewood earlier, and have a quantity of frozen and dried caribou as well as dried fish which the women use to make stews and soups. Each day that passes is longer than the previous one, which is a sign that the worst of Winter is over and the time for sealing is near.

Only the men will go sealing. We will be returning to our previous camp beside the sea while the women stay here. Bogodorasook says the ice pack sometimes brings harp seals to the bay beyond the islands. If not, we will travel the coast in search of harbour seals. In addition to dried meat and sealing weapons, we will be carrying our sleeping furs and a few skins. We won't be using a tent but will make ourselves a shelter of spruce boughs instead. We'll load our goods onto the wooden platforms we used to haul heavy loads.

When Bogodorasook began talking about the seal hunt a few days ago, I cut down a spruce tree, stripped off the bark and tried to shape the wood into skis. I thought hauling the platform on skis would make our journey easier. I also wanted skis for my feet. I'm used to travelling on skis, not snowshoes. But the stone tools wouldn't shape the skis I wanted and I burned the wood instead.

When the morning of our departure comes, seven of us put on snowshoes and set out, pulling our loads. By now, the storm snow has become firm and easy to walk on. Even so, we don't make it to the bay the first day but hunker down in the woods around a fire and doze through the night. Bogodorasook tells us to dream of seals.

At noon the next day, we reach our previous camp beside the sea. Immediately we see that an east wind has brought the pack ice shoreward, and that there are harp seals beyond the islands in the bay. The seals are so close the pups can be heard mewling for their mothers who have taken to the water to fish. We can't see the pups since they are as white as the ice but we can see the grey heads of the adults in the water. The fur of the harp seals is much sought after by the Norwegians, the pups especially. Their white fur is used to make muffs and foot warmers for highborn women. I went sealing with Thorvard and his men in Leifsbudir for the first time last Winter and am eager to return to the ice.

Bogodorasook says we must first cut spruce boughs and make a shelter. We also cut firewood and lay a fire. Then each of us collects his gear—a club, a tog-gling harpoon, a knife, a coil of deerhide rope—and we set out across the ice.

It's clear and cold, the east wind brisk and strong. At first, walking is easy, for the shore ice is smooth and flat. But farther out, past the islands, the shore ice has been pushed up by the pack ice into ridges and frozen. The seals are farther out than they look from the shore, scattered on ice pans floating here and there. The pups are birthed near water where the mothers can easily slip into the sea to fish. The ice pans are stained with blood from the birthing; most of the pups are a few days old. Before we reach the pups, Bogodorasook touches my arm and says, "No man kills more than he can haul back to camp."

"That's no more than two each," I protest. "Last winter we Greenlanders took four times that number."

"That's our way. If you can't honour it, you must return to camp," he says and resumes the lead.

I follow close behind, not wanting to separate myself from the others since any of us could easily slip and disappear beneath the ice. Walking becomes more difficult. We've reached the place where old ice has rafted onto new making jagged outcroppings and pinnacles that are treacherous to cross since there is often a patch of slush on the other side. One wrong step could plunge any of us into ice water. I know because I slipped into the water last winter and was rescued by Thorvard.

When they see us coming, a few of the mother seals take to the water where the males have been all along, but most of the mothers stay with their pups to protect them. Because the seals are on ice pans, we must cross open water to reach them. Fortunately most of the openings are narrow cracks. The dark lines of water look as though ropes have been flung across the ice. There are so many seals on the pans that I doubt we'll use our harpoons. Harpoons are used when seals are hunted in the water.

We begin the kill, clubbing the seals over the head to stun them, then finishing them off with a knife. It doesn't take me long to kill two seals which is all I can haul. I cut a hole in each seal's neck and pull deer rope through the holes to make a handle for hauling. Then I look around. All along I've been aware of the others nearby who have been working in pairs. As the seventh hunter I've been working alone. The other hunters have also killed their seals and have them ready for hauling. I notice each man has two seals except for Zathrasook and his father Boasook who have three each. Because of their heavier load, they choose to follow the others ashore. As the odd one out I am last. Zathrasook is between me and his father.

The wind shifts to the South. The shift makes walking more dangerous for us, for a change in the wind rearranges the ice, widening the cracks until new openings appear where there were none before. We come to the outcroppings of ice and slow down in

order to haul our loads over these ridges. One of the
rope handles breaks as I pull it uphill, and I stoop to
mend it. Deer rope isn't nearly as strong as the walrus
rope we use in Greenland. When I look up, all I can
see is the back of Boasook's head and shoulders. He's
disappeared over an ice ridge. I can't see Zathrasook
at all. Leaving my seals, I climb a large chunk of
upthrust ice and look down. Below me, I see
Zathrasook floundering in a pool of slush. I clamber
down, grab him by the hair and, grunting with effort,
heave him onto the ice. His seals have disappeared
into the slush. I shout to the others for help.

Fortunately Zathrasook hasn't swallowed any water
but his lips are blue and his teeth clack together as his
body shudders with cold. If he had stayed in the water
any longer, he would have been unable to stay afloat.
I rub his arms to help the blood move more quickly
inside. I don't think he knows it's me, either that, or
he's beyond caring who touches him. Now his father
is beside us. He urges Zathrasook to move his arms
and legs. Zathrasook obeys him and soon they begin
walking carefully ashore. I follow behind. When we
reach smoother ice, I leave my own seals and go back
for Boasook's which he has left on a ridge.

When I reach the camp, a huge fire is blazing.
Zathrasook sits close to it, wrapped in furs. How prudent of Bogodorasook to insist on laying the fire
before we began hunting. After we've warmed ourselves, we sculpt the seals, scraping the fat from the

skin and separating out the meat. By the time we're finished, all of us are tired from our work, and after eating seal meat we had set to roast earlier, we lie on the spruce boughs, too weary for telling a story of the hunt. I close my eyes and think about the Winter in Leifsbudir when we Greenlanders killed so many seals. The story of that hunt and the red men we chased down afterwards was told many times around our hearth fires and my memory of it comes back to me now as a dream.

Thorvard and the other Greenlanders, myself included, are on the ice. We've been sealing for several days. We want to get in one last day of sealing before the wind turns and takes the ice pack away. The wind holds for the morning, long enough for us to make another large kill.

The seals are hauled ashore. After sculpting and disembowelling them, we pile the carcasses on the ground outside the storage hut. Among us, we Greenlanders have killed such a quantity of seals that the hut is full of fresh meat.The new carcasses have to be stored outside, on the roof. The air is frosty enough that the meat won't spoil.

The next morning when Freydis goes out to the hut to get food for our morning meal, she sees Awadasut coming toward her, holding a spear. Freydis backs up against the hut and shouts for her husband, Thorvard. While she watches, Awadasut hoists a seal from the roof of the hut, and carrying it on his shoulders, starts to run across the meadow. Freydis yells, "Skraeling! Skraeling!" until Thorvard comes. Freydis points in the direction of the meadow and her husband looks up and sees Awadasut running away with a seal. Immediately, Thorvard comes inside the house and wakes us up, urging us to give chase. Dressing quickly, I pick up my axe, go outside and begin to run.

Ahead of me I see Awadasut running across the meadow. Beneath my feet the ground is thickly grown with osiers and bog laurel in which snow has caught and deepened. Because Awadasut is carrying the seal, he cannot run as fast as me. I can see he is losing ground. Behind me I hear Thorvard shouting and I force myself to run harder. Despite the pain in my chest which burns from the cold, I remain clear-headed enough to notice that Awadasut has some distance to go before he reaches the woods. Without turning, he drops the seal. Still I give chase. I know I can catch him. Soon I am within striking distance and throw my axe.

I wake up suddenly, shivering with cold. It's still dark. There are stars in the sky and the embers of the fire glow orange. But the fire offers no comfort. The dream was too real to go away. Once the story of the chase was more real than the dream, but that has changed. Since I learned that the red man I ran down was Awadasut, the story is not the same. A reshaping has taken place, I think in dreams. These dreams have occurred without my knowing. There is no other way to explain how my thoughts have changed. The word skraeling, which Freydis shouted, now has no meaning for me. For most of my life I used that word to describe someone like Awadasut as a wretch. Ignorance and fear shaped the word's meaning, not the truth.

I know Awadasut's death will continue to inhabit my dreams for some time to come, perhaps for years, but I am no longer discouraged by this. Just as I am learning to carve something useful with wood, so I am learning to make something from my thoughts that will better explain the truth. To do this I must learn how to see the difference between what I am now to what I once was. At the time of Awadasut's death I had thought his crime deserving of murder. It never occurred to me that I was the one committing the crime. That was because we Greenlanders thought that once we killed a seal, it belonged to us. Even though we had far more seal meat than we needed, most of it was kept inside the shed under lock and key, to prevent thralls and Icelanders from stealing it. Stealing is a serious crime among Norsemen. If a thrall is caught stealing something small, he's likely to lose an ear or a hand; if he's caught stealing livestock even a freeman can be killed on the spot.

That's not the way of these people. The Osweet don't own their goods in the same way Norsemen do. Stealing is unknown to them. At least I've never heard them use a word with that meaning. I doubt

Zathrasook thought that taking my ptarmigan was stealing. I think he was playing a trick, to keep me in my place.

As for owning goods, I have noticed many times how often the Osweet exchange tools and weapons and clothes. After my capture no one wore my clothes, but recently Tisewsut has taken to wearing my shoes and my robe. When I see him with these things, I wear his. I like this exchange; it makes me feel less like an outsider. Often I see girls and young women wearing one another's garments. If Gunnhild wore my mother's clothes, she would be punished. My father punishes Erling and Magnus for taking what isn't theirs. But with my captors, the situation is different. If no one owns anything, it's impossible to steal.

The morning we return to our winter camp, we load the skins, meat and fat onto the sleds with our gear and pull them through the woods and along the frozen river. The weather holds clear and we arrive at the mamateek halfway through the second day.

After we've rested a few days, we go to the coast again, for a second hunt. By then the wind has shifted the ice pack too far offshore for us to hunt harp seals. Instead we travel South to look for harbour seals which are much more easy to hunt since they whelp their pups on the rocky shore. We find seals less than half a morning's walk from our camp. There are fewer than thirty seals altogether but we manage to kill four. That wouldn't be enough to satisfy Greenlanders, but it satisfies Bogodorasook and the others.

That night when we are gathered around the campfire Bogodorasook says, "It seems Wobee's presence is helping us, for winter hunting goes far better for us this year than it did the last when there were no seals around here at all."

"I'm pleased to be of some help, after the grief I've caused," I say. "It would take a lifetime of help, and I still could not make up for his loss."

This is the first time I've spoken aloud about Awadasut and the part I played in his death.

"You speak well," Bogodorasook says. "I am pleased that you are learning to think like the Osweet." The others nod their heads in agreement. As expected, Zathrasook gives no indication he has heard. Perhaps he does not like the thought that a wretch like me has saved his life.

13

Before we return to our woodland camp, I ask Bogodorasook about hunting walrus. Twice last Winter, Thorvard and I saw walrus near Leifsbudir about this time of year. We were rowing across the bay in sight of Leif's houses when two walrus floated past on ice pans. Like harbour seals, walrus whelp ashore. If we could kill walrus along this shore, I could make the kind of rope we used in Greenland. Walrus rope is far stronger than the deerhide rope the Osweet use. Norwegians pay a high price for walrus rope which they use to rig their ships. The Osweet have no ships but I'm sure they could find many uses for walrus rope.

"The big walrus herds are far from here," Bogodorasook tells me. He points West. "On the other coast, across the inland sea. Sometimes we hunt them there. Not often."

"Are there any on this coast?"

"A few."

I tell him I would like to try to find one so that I can make some rope from its hide. Bogodorasook doesn't object. "Shawbawsut and Hathasut will go with you," he says, "the others will stay here with me. If you don't find walrus today, they'll be too far away to hunt. If you don't return tonight, we'll know you have found walrus and will be here tomorrow."

Shawbawsut, Hathasut and I set out, snowshoeing South over the shore ice which has a skiff of fresh snow on top. It's faster going on the ice than along the shore. We cross the inlet where we hunted harbour seals yesterday. Some of the herd have returned and are lying on the rocks. Further on, we pass a second inlet and more harbour seals. When we stop to eat our midday meal of dried caribou, we hear a sea bull bellowing somewhere to the South.

The walrus aren't far. In fact, they're just beyond a steep, rocky promontory that juts out from the land ahead. The slope gives us an advantage, allowing us to come up to the walrus from behind and take them by surprise. Carrying our harpoons, spears and knives, we leave our snowshoes on the shore at the foot of the slope and begin climbing the icy rocks. It's slow going since we must be careful where we place our feet. At the top, we look down the other side and see about thirty walrus stretched out on the rocks below. They're facing a cove of open water. Near the shore, there's a spring bubbling into the sea.

It isn't a large herd but this makes no difference to us since we'll slaughter only one walrus. Sea cattle are such huge beasts that one walrus is all we can handle. Fortunately, we're downwind from the herd so there's little chance of the walrus catching our scent. Before we make a move, we choose a walrus. In unison we charge down the rocky slope and throw our harpoons. Mine hits its target but hangs partway out of the walrus's flank. The toggle hasn't gone deep enough to take hold of the fat inside. But Shawbawsut's and Hathasut's toggles hold. The walrus is so large that she drags them forward as she heaves her bulk toward the water. By now the other walrus are bellowing and clambering over each other in an effort to escape. Unless we can drag the walrus away from the others, we'll be in the middle of the heaving mass of flesh. I remember hearing about Greenlanders who were crushed and gored by escaping walrus. Hathasut plunges his spear into the walrus and holds her down while Shawbawsut severs the neck with a knife.

Now we face the task of getting the walrus over the promontory. It takes three of us pushing, prodding, pulling and tugging to get the carcass up the slope. Once we are on the top, we give the carcass a shove and it rolls down the other side. By now, the sky has become low and dark.

"We'll never make it back to the others before dark," Shawbawsut says. "We'll have to camp somewhere nearby for the night."

We put on our snowshoes and begin to haul the walrus along the shore, Shawbawsut leading. He strikes an inland course toward the woods.

"We'll camp here where the Aswan won't see us."

"Who are the Aswan?"

"Seal people who come from the North on the ice," Shawbawsut says. "They're fierce fighters who try to take our women. We avoid them whenever we can."

"There are also white bears to think of," Hathasut says. "At this time of year, they sometimes come this far South. We Osweet usually avoid them, preferring to leave them for our brothers, the Washawet, to hunt."

Hathasut and I build a shelter of spruce boughs while Shawbawsut takes out the fire stone and makes a fire. We cut open the walrus and remove the heart and liver which we skewer for roasting. While the meat is cooking, we cut away the ivory tusks and gut and skin the walrus. We leave the carcass some distance from the fire so it will freeze, but close enough so that if wolves should come, the carcass can be hauled close to the fire with ropes. Hathasut says that if a white bear comes, not to pull on the ropes, for the bear is just as likely to eat us as the walrus, a fact Greenlanders know well. Fortunately, no bears or wolves appear and the night passes peacefully enough.

Late next morning, we reach Bogodorasook and the others. As soon as we've rejoined them, we begin the journey back to our winter camp. With so much fresh meat, Bogodorasook says, it will take us longer to return than it did to come.

We arrive at the mamateek late on the second day.

The women are pleased to see us, though our arrival means they have days of hard work ahead of them scraping and cleaning skins.

Early the next morning I begin scraping the walrus hide. Behind my back the women nudge each other and laugh. The men cannot pass me by without making a joke about my doing women's work. I ignore the teasing, wanting to make the rope on my own. With only one walrus to work with, I cannot afford to make a mistake. For the next few days I spend all my time cleaning, cutting and braiding the hide until I've made a large coil of walrus rope. One evening when everyone is inside, I make a show of handing Bogodorasook the rope.

"It's stout rope," I tell him. "Very strong."

Bogodorasook takes the rope and smiles. He holds out the end to me, then grips the rope further along the coil.

"Pull," he says and I do.

Back and forth we pull, testing the rope.

"It's good rope," he says. "I'm pleased you made it."

"Now I will try it," Zathrasook says. He gets up and takes the end of the rope and tugs until I pull. Back and forth we tug, each of us tugging harder than before. I know Zathrasook is trying to jerk me off my feet. I decide to be as hard on him as he is on me. I give the rope a mighty tug, hoping to pull Zathrasook off his feet. He lets go. I lose my balance and stumble backwards, narrowly missing the fire. There's nothing to hold onto to break my fall and I keep on going through the tent flap and land flat on my back in the snow. I get up quickly, stick my head around the flap and hold up my end of the rope.

"You see how strong this rope is," I shout. "It can knock a man into the snow!"

I laugh with the others. I want Zathrasook to know that he has a way to go before he'll get the better of me.

14

More than a year has passed since Awadasut's death. We are now in the time between seasons; it's neither cold enough to be Winter, nor warm enough to be Summer. It's a time of rain. The rain has washed away the snow leaving a sodden mass of brown leaves and spruce needles on the forest floor. The ice on the lake is grey where it's rotted through. The sky is as heavy as lead. The world seems colourless and dead; even the evergreens seem lifeless.

One morning we waken to find our world transformed. Overnight the wind has brought a glitter storm. Everywhere the rain has frozen onto the branches and trees, sheathing them in ice. The clouds have lifted and the sun shines on the ice, making it glisten and wink. Every branch and twig, every needle and cone, every stick and stone is silvered by the sun. The slender stalks of grass shine like silver threads.

Once I noticed Leif Eiriksson's wife, Jorunn, wearing a pair of brooches that a silversmith had made by shaping fine silver threads into tiny flowers and leaves. She wore the brooches, as Greenland women do, on either side of her chest. When I come out of our mamateek in the morning and see the silver thaw, I think of those brooches. It's a magical morning. Like the others who have come outside, I am delighted by this glistening world. The silver shines so brightly it waters my eyes.

By midday the sun has melted the ice and the brilliance has gone, leaving the woods fresh and moist, the colours brighter than they were before. After the long hours inside the mamateek—it's been too rainy to light a fire outside—all of us are eager to be up and about. Some of the men go off to set snares, but I choose to sit on a log and carve. I'm making a comb for Abidith, using the wood of a birch I found near the lake. The comb is harder to carve than the spoon. Only now am I finishing the comb's teeth which have been difficult to make. Soon I will be ready to carve the handle. I intend to take my time with this for I will carve my feelings for Abidith into the design, and want to give her my very best work.

During the winter months, I have become very fond of Abidith, as fond of her as I am of my sister though in a different way. One day Abidith asks me if I have brothers and sisters and I tell her about Gunnhild, Magnus and Erling. She wants me to describe them, as well as my parents and the place where we live. Another time she asks me to tell her about the ship that brought the Greenlanders across the ocean. I describe the ship and tell her it was named the *Vinland*.

"But the ship is gone now," I tell her. "It sank last

winter, after it became frozen in pack ice."

"Why was it named the *Vinland*?"

"Vinland is a country on this side of the water." I tell her about Leif Eiriksson's voyage to Vinland, how he travelled Southwest and found a country which was warmer than Leifsbudir and had luxuries the Greenlanders favoured such as grapes and honey. "I've never been to Vinland myself but I'm told there are beaches of white sand and warm water. Game is so plentiful no one needs to hunt. The trees yield sweet fruits of various kinds. The weather is summery all year round."

"It doesn't sound real to me," Abidith says.

"Leif Eiriksson thought it was," I say. "And that's good enough for me."

Though I didn't hear her telling Bogodorasook about Vinland, Abidith must have mentioned it to him for soon after I've spoken to her about it, one day Bogodorasook asks me to tell the others about Vinland. I tell them the little I know. Then they want me to describe the ship named the *Vinland* that brought me across the sea.

"It's much longer than your canoes," I say. "It will hold all of us with room to spare. It has a tree in the middle with a piece of cloth attached. The cloth is large, about the size of six or eight caribou skins sewn together. It fills with wind and pushes the boat along."

I go on to describe how the ship's keel is carved from a large tree, how boards are nailed to make the sides, how the knees and crossbeams are put in place and the planking laid on top. I tell them it takes a lot of tree wood to make a ship and that we don't have tree wood in Greenland.

Bogodorasook says he thinks it strange that people should rely so much on goods from far away.

No one asks about the voyage which is just as well. I prefer not to think about the crossing which was so storm driven and unlucky that I never expected to see land again. Even so, the memory of that dangerous voyage sometimes slips unbidden into my mind.

Off the coast of Helluland the sky became as dark as night. Thick clouds blocked the sun. The wind blew the ship seaward and we Greenlanders lost sight of land. The swells became so massive that we could only see the swell we were in, and halfway up the next.

We lost track of time, which was to say the light. Nor could we navigate. The sunstone Leif Eiriksson gave our helmsman, Evyind, was useless. There was no moon or stars.

The waves became steeper, looming above the ship like Greenland's fells. The shifting mountains were so high, their valleys so deep, that the ship couldn't shape itself to the water but faltered perilously on the summits, groaning as if it would break in two. Each time the ship was stranded on a wave top, a sickness rose in my throat then slowly sank to my belly as the ship plunged into a trough. I gave up eating since nothing I ate would stay down. Nor could I use the privy pails which had long since been knocked over. My clothes stank of vomit and piss. The entire ship reeked with foul odours, most of which came from the hold where the animals stood in swill of stinking dung.

Waves broke over the ship. One of them snapped the rope securing the water barrels. Another wave washed over the deck sweeping away one of the goats that had got loose, and a man named Lopt.

Through all this I held onto the mast where the others were tied. The storm continued unabated, how long none of us knew. It could have been two days, it could have been four or five. However long it was, it seemed to take forever before the storm finally moved on...

One day when I am sitting by the fire concentrating on the comb and remembering the voyage, Abidith, who without my knowing it, has been quietly slipping hot rocks into a container of soup, startles me by saying, "It seems your memory of the voyage is so terrible it follows you around."

I know that she has somehow guessed my thoughts, not in every detail perhaps, but she has learned enough to gain a certain power over me. Again, I feel as naked and helpless as a newborn child, for I am reminded that while she knows my innermost thoughts, I do not know hers. Though I have tried many times, I have been unable to persuade her to tell me about herself. Instead, she urges me to tell her about my people and especially enjoys hearing tales about the god Thor who is forever getting into trouble with giants and other folk. When I ask Abidith to tell me Osweet tales in return, she smiles and turns her head away.

"You know more about me than I do about you," I tell her.

"How can that be?" she says. "You are here with me and my family now. Yet I have never seen your people."

I have decided to carve a ship on the handle of Abidith's comb. The ship will hold my dreams. Though I'll carve an outline much like the *Vinland*'s, I won't think of the ship as belonging to Leif Eiriksson. This will be a new ship built especially for Abidith and me. This ship will never be caught in a storm. It will never be held on top of a mountainous wave, or plunge into a deep trough. This ship will sail on gentle swells that will take us to a milder land. With Abidith beside me, I will be seeking Vinland. Abidith will likely guess the feelings I am carving into the comb. She will know the dream I have for her and me. Strangely this does not trouble me. In fact it is what I want, for I doubt I will be able to tell her my feelings any other way.

Abidith and I are sailing South to Vinland, to the land of honey and grapes, where exotic fruits tumble from the trees, and nuts of many kinds fall into waiting hands. There is honeycomb in the hollow of an oak and a fountain of fresh spring water. There are mussels and lobsters aplenty and in the woods grouse and deer. Unsown wheat grows along the shore.

Abidith pounds the wheat and mixes it with honey to make sweet cakes. I make us a shelter on the beach and roof it with woven leaves. The air is scented with wild pea blossoms. The sun always shines. We shed our winter clothes and lie about on the sand. When we grow hot we slip into the shallow water to cool off. Around us the world shimmers with promise and light.

Four

15

The in between season has passed. The ice on the lake and along the stream has melted and the alders and birches are in bud. The buds are tight and the evenings cool, but soon the trees will be leafing out and the grass will be green. Before this happens, we Osweet will be on our way to the sea. Every year at this time, clouds of black flies arrive at our camp in the woods. No matter how well ochred we are, the flies find ways to bite our skin. They crawl through our hair to our scalps, they fly into our ears and noses, they hover around our eyes and lips. Later, on hot summer days, the mosquitoes attack with stingers that stab through the ochre and grease. To avoid these invasions, we travel to the coast where sea breezes keep away the worst of the flies.

When we left our winter camp last year, we travelled to our summer camp beside the eastern sea. But this year when we leave our winter camp, we will be travelling in the opposite direction, to the place on the western sea that lies between two lands and is called the Creator's Toe. That is where, every two years, the gathering of our people takes place. The

Owasposhno-un will come from the South, bringing supplies of ochre and fur. The Washawet will come from the North, bringing a supply of arrow stone and white bear fur. We Osweet will bring caribou fur and bone, as well as black bear furs. At the summer gathering, our families will trade what we have. All of us depend on the caribou, and all of us live where there is a supply of birch-bark. But some of us have more of these goods than others and bring them along to trade. There will be a naming and ochring ceremony and new marriages will be made. Ever since the Creator shot his arrows into the ground, these gatherings have taken place. The length of the summer gathering will depend on the abundance of food. With so many of us living in one place, there are many mouths to feed. It will depend on the supply of shellfish and caplin. If the caplin run is strong our stay will be long.

The time is nearly here when I must choose either Watsut of the Owasposhno-un, or Koorsook of the Washawet for a husband. Whoever it will be, he will live with my family for a month after which, I will live a month with his. If we suit each other after this, we will marry two years from this Summer. Two years seems like a long time to me, but it is what I prefer; I'm not ready to marry yet. I know when I do, I will have to live with my husband's family. Because the Osweet have a shortage of men, I will have to leave our family. I can't bear the thought of leaving

Grandmother and Grandfather, my father and mother and my sister, the new baby.

The ochring ceremony will take place midsummer. Grandmother says with a new supply of ochre, Wobee will probably be ochred, but his ochring won't be part of the ceremony which is known only to our people.

"Wobee has learned much about our ways," Grandmother says. "I'm pleased with him. But I don't think he feels himself to be one of us yet."

"Maybe he never will," I say. "He often dreams of getting away." I don't tell her about the dreams Wobee has of going away with me to the place called Vinland.

"That's to be expected," Grandmother says. "If any of us was to be captured and taken to Wobee's land, we would also dream of returning home."

I have seen the picture of Wobee's home in the place he calls Greenland, a picture he keeps inside his head and which he's used to describe the country where he lived with his parents, his sister and his brothers. The hut is long and low and built of stone. There's a hearth down the middle where the cooking is done. The fire is usually fed with twigs and turf which makes the room smoky, even in Summer. In Winter it's dark all the time and seal oil lamps are used for light and heat. Outside, there's a lake that runs all the way to the sea and is filled with ice. Even in Summer there's ice. Behind the hut, the ground slopes upward toward cliffs and mountain valleys filled with snow and ice. Everywhere Wobee looks there are stones, but no trees.

I tell Grandmother that I wouldn't want to live in Wobee's land, which is blue and white. "I wouldn't want to travel in his boat though it's much bigger than ours, even if it took me to a place he calls Vinland."

A sly smile appears on Grandmother's lips. "It seems you have become close to Wobee," she says.

I tell her I have merely been doing what Grandmother urged me to do, which is true.

Our journey to the coast will be by water and land. There will be a day's journey by lake and then another day's journey overland during which we will carry our canoes West to the inland sea. Once we reach the sea, we will have a two-day paddle South along the coast before we reach our gathering place. The men often say that if they were travelling alone, they could make the coastal journey in a day, that we women and children slow them down. The men are joking when they tell us this. They know the summer gathering would mean little without their wives and daughters.

While the mamateek is being taken down, the canoes are carried to the lake and our goods stored inside. This includes the hides and furs we intend to trade. Finally we are ready and get into the canoes. My mother and I sit on a pile of sleeping skins at the back, Messee between my knees. Dysee and the new baby sit at the opposite end. My father and Hathasut paddle, my father at the front, Hathasut near me at the back. Wobee is also travelling in our canoe. Sometimes he takes a turn with a paddle. Whenever Wobee sits in Hathasut's place, because of the crowding, his hip is braced against my knees. When he brings the paddle back, his elbow touches my arm. I don't like this arrangement, but it doesn't make me angry in a way it would have earlier. In my own way I have become used to Wobee.

Because the canoes are so low in the water, our progress is slow. The first night, we get no further than the end of the lake. We camp on the shore, in a clearing surrounded by woods. As long as I can remember, we've camped around this circle of fire-blackened stones, beneath the protective branches of spruce. The spruce are so tall their lower branches have long since been removed to make space for a camp. The night is clear and mild. It doesn't look like rain but at this time of year, no one can be sure when the weather will change. After we have eaten some dried caribou meat, we choose our sleeping places in the circle, feet pointing toward the fire. Wobee chooses a place beside me.

As we are falling asleep, the wind begins to rise. It's a south wind that brings the lightest of rains. The rain makes us shift restlessly in our sleep. We pull the flaps of our sleeping covers over our heads. The wind moves between the trees, making them sigh and moan. I soon become aware that Wobee has been snared by a bad dream.

He's deep in a forest. Giant trees loom overhead. The trees sway in the breeze. They rock from side to side. Their limbs creak and groan. They bend at the waist and their long arms reach out, crawling over the ground. They move across the grassy clearing, probing each sleeper until they find Wobee's place. They move over his sleeping form, groping beneath the deerskin covering until they find his face. The tree fingers are rough and sharp. They scratch his skin. They poke into his nose, pushing so hard they stop his breath. He opens his mouth to shout, but the fingers reach inside and grab his tongue.

Beside me, I hear Wobee moving his head from side to side, fighting to get his breath, trying to free his tongue. I reach out and pat his arm. I remind him that it's only a bad dream.

I can feel Wobee gradually coming awake; the tree giants are letting him go. I continue patting his arm until his breathing stills and he's calmed himself. Then I turn on my side and pull the sleeping cover over my head, thinking how strange it is that someone so impressed with wooden boats should be afraid of trees.

Early next morning, we break camp in the drizzling rain and continue our journey on foot. This means carrying our canoes and gear through forest scrub and swamp. There's a trail we follow each time we make the journey to the summer gathering, but in some places it is blocked by deadfall and the men must go

ahead to make sure the trail is clear. When they are
satisfied it is, the men return to help carry gear and
trading goods. From time to time, the youngest children must be carried, which means there's a good deal
of doubling back to pick up goods that have been set
down along the trail when a child has been lifted onto
a shoulder or back. In spite of these difficulties, by
evening we have reached the water. This is an inland
sea between two lands. In the West, the opposite
shore is blurred. It lies like a sleeping animal in the
rain. We arrange our sleeping places around the circle
of fire-blackened stones above a rocky beach. Again,
Wobee makes his sleeping place beside me.

Tonight Wobee sleeps peacefully until dawn. When
all of us have risen and eaten our share of dried meat,
we continue our journey by canoe. We paddle over
shoals and around a large rocky shoulder that shrugs
sideways into the sea. On the other side of the shoulder are many islands and rocks. We paddle from one
island to another, twice going ashore to rest. Once we
stop to fish. The cod have returned to these waters
and are easily caught. That night, we camp around
another circle of fire-blackened stones on the largest
island and roast our fish.

"We'll reach the Creator's Toe before noon tomorrow," Grandfather says. By this he means the place
where the Creator stood when he shot his arrows that
made the people. It's here that the first arrows from
which the ancient ones sprang are buried.

Watsut's family, the Owasposhno-un, will already be there when we arrive. They always arrive first. That's because they don't have to journey overland, but only need follow the coastline North in their canoes. The Washawet always arrive last, since they have the longest distance to travel, living as they do in the Northwest. They must travel South, cross the inland sea, then follow the coast along. I have never been to the land of the Washawet where Koorsook lives, but Grandfather was there once hunting walrus.

As we draw nearer the meeting place, I can't stop myself from thinking of Watsut. Now that he's a man, he'll be taller and wider shouldered than he was two summers ago. I hope he hasn't changed too much, that I will find as much about him to like as I did two summers ago. If I have to live apart from my family, I would prefer to marry into the Owasposhno-un since they live so much closer to us than the Washawet.

When we are near the Creator's Toe, I can see the summer mamateeks, four altogether. There are at least twenty Owasposhno-un standing along the shore, waiting to welcome us.

Their leader, Gwanesh, wades into the water to welcome Grandfather and Grandmother. Gwanesh is the only old one here, his wife Schoon having died four winters ago. Our canoe comes in last which gives me time to scan the shore for Watsut. I don't see him. But I see the figure of a tall man with a bony chest and shoulders. He isn't at all like Watsut. He's someone I haven't seen before. For some reason I can't stop staring at the man. There's something different about him, though from this distance I don't know exactly what it is. I look away searching one person after another until I find Watsut. He has left the others and is standing alone near the canoes, perhaps so I will notice him more. It's a relief to see that he looks much the same, not as tall as I expected but much thicker in the arms and chest. As we near the shore I notice the whale's tail around Watsut's neck which means he's earned the right to wear the Owasposhno-un totem since I saw him last.

When our canoe has glided to a stop, Watsut wades into the water and comes to steady it. He doesn't look at me but he knows exactly where I am. When I step from the canoe carrying Messee, Watsut reaches out and takes the child from my arms. He swings her out of the canoe. I step onto the beach and he turns to me and says,

"I notice Dysee has a new child."

"Yes. This year we've brought a son to the gathering."

"My sister has also brought a son. Now we number fifteen men and ten women."

I know Watsut's mentioning the numbers to tell me that he's thinking of me as his wife; that if we marry, I will be expected to live with his people, since there's a shortage of women among the Owasposhno-un. Even so, I say, more to tease than anything else, "That means you have men to spare to help our family."

He laughs, showing strong white teeth and wrinkles at the corners of his eyes. I remember Watsut always laughed with his eyes.

"Where's Awadasut?" he says. "I see you've brought a white man with you but I don't see your brother."

"The Winter after our last gathering he was killed by white men." I point to Wobee. "He threw the weapon that stunned Awadasut when he was running with a seal."

For a long time Watsut doesn't reply. At last he says, "So my friend is gone." My brother was two years older than Watsut and in Watsut's eyes could do no wrong.

I tell him Wobee was captured in exchange.

"We've done the same," Watsut says. He nods toward the tall bony figure I saw earlier. "Beneath the red ochre is a white man. We call him Cheething because he looks like a stick."

Although the name is meant to be funny, neither of us laughs. How serious we have become. Two summers ago we would have laughed at Cheething's name and run off to skip flat stones on the water, or search for limpets and crabs among the rocks.

"Let's walk on the long beach," Watsut says, "and you can tell me how Awadasut died."

The long beach behind the encampment is where two summers ago we used to come to play. To reach it, we cross a mossy plateau broken by juniper bushes. We come to the place of the stones. This is a wide rocky platform on the same level as the sea. Here and there on the platform are huge rounded stones on which our people sit when they come to watch a dancer perform. Watsut and I cross the platform and come to a beach of coarse grey sand. Running the length of the beach is a long pile of driftwood. Here, where for as long as anyone can remember the tide has brought in all manner of driftwood, Watsut and I spent many happy days as children, making a game of guessing what the different driftwood shapes might be. "This is an owl" we might say, or "that is a stag." "Over there is an eagle sweeping down for a kill." Or "See the bear standing on his hind legs?" There was no end to the shapes we saw sculpted in the wood.

Today we sit on a log that resembles nothing but itself, an uprooted tree. I tell Watsut the circumstances of my brother's death. It is a relief to speak of it at last, for as I speak, some of the bitterness I feel toward Wobee ebbs away. "Zathrasook and the others brought the body home. We built Awadasut a grave on the island of birches."

When I finish the telling, Watsut and I sit for a time, silently staring at the water. We are thinking much the same thing, that Awadasut's body is surrounded by the sea, safe from evil spirit snatchers. Evil spirits don't cross water which means my brother can lie in peace.

Watsut breaks the silence.

"Do you remember at our last gathering we told the tale of what happened to Ashoo and Anuit, how a year before, some white men killed them when they went to empty the flounder traps along the shore?"

"I remember it well."

"That story was unfinished," Watsut says, then goes on, "for soon after we left here and returned South, six of us went into the woods and came across four white men hunting in the place where our winter camp had been long ago, back in the days when Gwanesh's father was alive. The white men didn't see us and for a long time we stalked them instead of caribou. It was clear the white men weren't used to hunting in the woods. Two of them lost themselves from the others. As the night shadows grew longer, we talked about what we should do with the lost white hunters. Obditch wanted to kill them and cut off their heads; Ashoo had been his brother. But the rest of us spoke against doing this. My father said he was curious about the white men. He thought we should capture both of them and take them back to our camp alive. But as we were dragging the men through the bush, one of them tried to escape and Obditch slit his throat. Then he cut off his head and brought it back on a spear."

"The Osweet have never done that," I say.

"Nor did the Owasposhno-un until then," Watsut says. "But Obditch and some others said the time for sparing an enemy's life was past."

"But Cheething's still alive."

"Yes, he came willingly enough. Later, when we reached our camp, he drew a picture in the earth of a large boat with men in it at the end of the bay near where we'd been hunting. My father and I and two others returned there, but the boat and the men were gone. They left behind a forest of stumps. Cheething said it was trees they had mainly come for, not game. After he learned our language, Cheething told us many things about the white men who, he says, live on islands far to the North across the water. He says there are many more of them than those who came here. My father says it will be wise of us to make Cheething one of us so that he can help us to learn about the white men so we'll know what to do about them if they come back."

"If they come back, we had better find a safe place to hide." I shiver, though not with cold.

"Obditch is against keeping Cheething," Watsut says. "He wants him dead."

"Zathrasook wants Wobee dead."

"Gwanesh says we'll discuss the matter this Summer after all of us have been gathered here a while. He says there's something to be said on both sides. After everyone has spoken, we'll decide what to do with the captives."

"I don't want our people to become man killers," I tell him. "I don't want Wobee's head on a spear."

"I don't either. A head looks best where it is," Watsut says and gives my hair a playful tug. "I look forward to the time when yours will rest on my shoulder at night." Then before I might think he's being too forward, Watsut points to a driftwood root shaped like a spearhead. "What would you say that is?"

"A mamateek."

"I say the fin of a killer whale."

We walk along the beach, pointing out one shape after another, disagreeing about each one, laughing easily as we did as children. Although Grandmother has warned me not to be hasty in choosing a husband, I can't help thinking I know who it will be.

FIVE

16

After we come ashore, I set to work helping the others unload our gear. Imamasduit and the women have already begun building the mamateeks. There will be three smaller mamateeks instead of one large one like the one we used all Winter. This is disappointing since it means I'll no longer be sharing a mamateek with Abidith and her family, but will live with Imamasduit and Bogodorasook as I did last Summer. While I help carry goods from the canoes, I look around for Abidith, wanting to talk to her, but she's nowhere in sight. Between them, Imamasduit and Bogodorasook keep me too busy to go in search of her.

Later in the evening, when we're eating roasted fish around the fire, a tall bony man comes to sit beside me.

"You're a Greenlander," he says in Norse.

Startled, I look up and see a blue-eyed man smiling at my surprise.

"I'm not a ghost," he says. "I used to be Jokul. I was one of the Icelanders who was abducted in the Bay of Maples nearly two years ago. Now I'm Cheething."

Had Jokul not spoken, I might not have recognized him. In the first place, he's covered from head to foot in greased ochre; even his hair is red. In the second place, because he's an Icelander, I hardly knew him. I remember seeing him once, at a feast soon after we Greenlanders arrived in Leifsbudir, but he took no notice of me. He was one of Helgi Egilsson's crew and had travelled to Norway many times as well as to the land of the Franks. A worldly man such as he had no time for a Greenland farmer's son. In any event, the Greenlanders and Icelanders didn't often mix in Leifsbudir; the Icelanders lived in a different house from us and except for wood-cutting expeditions, came and went on their own.

I remember the story about the disappearance of Jokul and Grimkel who, soon after we arrived in Leifsbudir, travelled South to the Bay of Maples with an expedition of men to harvest timber. Two Greenlanders, Thorvard and Falgeir, went to the woods with the Icelanders to hunt. The Icelanders, who were better sailors than hunters, got lost in the woods. When Thorvard and Falgeir went looking for them, they found Jokul's belt and Grimkel's shoe in a clearing, but they never found the men. Thorvard and Falgeir managed to get out of the woods alive. Afterwards, when they were trying to explain the disappearance of Jokul and Grimkel to the Icelanders, they said the two men must have been taken by invisible creatures since they had seen no one in the woods, except themselves. The Icelanders didn't believe a word of the Greenlanders' tale and said Thorvard and Falgeir had made up this fanciful story to cover up their own heinous crimes.

The fact that one of the lost Icelanders is now standing in front of me renders me speechless for a time. Finally I ask where Grimkel is.

"Grimkel's dead," Jokul says. "He tried to escape."

"So did I, but I'm alive."

Jokul says nothing to this. Instead he says, "Are you going to tell me who you are?"

"I'm Wobee," I say. "I mean, Thrand."

"I remember. You're one of the young men who came to Leifsbudir with his father."

"Yes, Ozur is my father's name."

"I didn't know your father. I was captured before the Icelanders became well acquainted with the Greenlanders."

"The Icelanders and Greenlanders never became well acquainted," I tell him. "There was a serious falling out. In the end the two camps avoided each other."

"Norsemen are always falling out with one another," Jokul says. "I must say I don't miss them much."

"Don't you miss your wife and family?" Jokul is probably twice my age.

"I have no wife. My only kin in Iceland was a sister who died years ago birthing a child."

"Do you know why you were captured?"

"At the time I didn't, but later on I came to understand. You remember the story about the voyage the Icelander Thorfinn Karlsefni made over here."

"All I know is that Thorfinn Karlsefni came to Leifsbudir several years ago with a large number of men. He returned to Greenland shortly before we left."

"While Thorfinn Karlsefni and his men were in these parts, they killed two of the Oswaposhno-un, Ashoo and Anuit. Struck them down cold bloodedly while they were trying to empty their flounder traps. Grimkel and I were taken in exchange for those men. It was expected that we would do the work these men had done so that their wives and children wouldn't be deprived, but as I said Grimkel was killed. Ashoo's wife Shanduit now lives with her brother whose wife died in a fall. I live with Anuit's widow Poorish. It's up to me to see that she and her children don't suffer from want."

"They allowed you to marry her?"

"Poorish and I aren't married. I merely live in her mamateek and do the work her husband did. The Owasposhno-un regard it as fair exchange for the hardship caused by Anuit's death."

"Then you're well treated."

"Yes, and you?"

"The same. I expected to be treated like a thrall but I do the same tasks as everyone else." I finish my fish and lick the grease off my hands.

When I next speak, though we're talking in Norse, I lower my voice, "I want to talk to you about a plan of escape." Of course I haven't been able to make a plan, but one can be worked out later and would include Abidith, of course.

"If you're asking me to escape with you," Jokul says, "forget it. I'm not going anywhere."

"Why?"

"I've told you. I like these people. I have no reason to leave."

I try another tack. "Weren't you one of the Icelanders who was building a pram in Leifsbudir?"

"I was."

"Could you help me build a pram I could use to escape?"

"Even if you and I lived close by, which we don't, it would take us a long time to build a pram with rock tools," Jokul says roughly. "If I were you, I'd give up the idea of escaping."

"That's easy to say when you have no kin at home. But I have my mother and father, my sister and brothers in Greenland."

"I don't say it will be easy," Jokul says, more softly than before. "But I think you should get used to the idea of staying here."

A little boy comes up to us. The boy tugs Jokul's hand and reminds him that he promised to take him fishing before the night is out. Jokul allows himself to be pulled to his feet.

After they've left, I sit for a long time, thinking about Jokul's advice. I think about my friend Teit. If he were sitting here instead of Jokul, he wouldn't think twice about helping me escape. Maybe I'm giving up on Jokul too soon. Maybe if Jokul could be made to understand how much I miss my family, and how much they must be missing me, he could be persuaded to help me. Before I settle inside the mamateek for the night, I resolve to talk to Jokul again soon.

17

The next day the Washawet arrive. These are red people from the North. As the Washawet beach their canoes and come ashore, I notice they number slightly more than the Osweet, there being eighteen of them including babies. The Washawet look much the same as the others, but instead of a bone ornament around their necks, the grown-ups wear a necklace of bear teeth. I examine the Washawet carefully to see if any of them might be white under their ochre. After the surprise of Jokul, it's possible the Washawet have also captured a white man from an earlier expedition. But there's no white man among them. One of the Washawet young women stares boldly at me, fascinated by my whiteness, I suppose. She's shorter and wider than Abidith, but not unpleasantly shaped.

I have hardly seen Abidith since we arrived and only then at a distance. Her parents' mamateek isn't next to ours but further along the beach. I miss having her close by. There's no more sleeping side by side, or talking together. I have been working hard on Abidith's comb. As soon as I finish carving the ship on the handle, which will be soon, I intend to give her the comb.

The grown-ups spend much of their time sitting around the outside fires, talking and laughing while the children tumble about like bear cubs. Often I see Abidith in the company of a young Owasposhno-un man.

Several days after the Washawet arrive, when Imamasduit and I are sitting outside, the old woman sees me watching Abidith and her companion walk along the shore. Abidith is laughing in a carefree way I've never seen before.

"The young man is Watsut." Imamasduit says. "He's living with Abidith's family now. He's the one she's chosen to be her husband."

My disappointment must show. Imamasduit puts her hand on my arm and gently says, "Because of Awadasut, Abidith could never be your mate." Then she says, "But there's someone else who might. From the way she watches you, I know she already has her eye on you."

I look around and see the Washawet young woman a short distance away, looking at me.

"That's Ahune," Imamasduit says.

I grumble about Ahune following me wherever I go.

"Then speak to her."

I have no intention of speaking to Ahune. If I cannot have Abidith for a companion, then I prefer to be alone.

"You won't be so lonely," Imamasduit says, giving

me one of her worn-toothed smiles, "if you have a mate."

Despite what Imamasduit says, I avoid Ahune. I dislike being followed. One day when I'm sitting on the beach working on Abidith's comb, Ahune approaches me from behind and catches me unawares.

"What's that you're making?" she asks.

"Nothing." I cover the comb with my hand. The carving is finished and I have been polishing it.

But she doesn't leave.

"Where you come from men must be afraid of women," she says.

"I'm not afraid."

"Then why do you run from me?"

"I don't run."

"Don't run too far. I have something to tell you. Tomorrow the old ones will be discussing you and the one they call Cheething."

"What do you mean?"

"Since we've never had white men live among us before, we must decide what to do with you. All the big decisions are made at the summer gatherings."

"What's there to decide?" I say carelessly though fear, like a frightened hare, has bolted into my chest.

"I told you," Ahune says, "they have to decide what to do with you and Cheething."

"But I thought they had already decided about me."

"The Osweet have, but our people also include the Owasposhno-un and the Washawet. They, too, must decide."

I take a better look at Ahune, trying to determine if she's someone I can trust. Why is she telling me this? She stares at me so openly that I think she must be speaking the truth.

"There's nothing to be afraid of," she says, "but I thought you should be warned in case you want to prepare yourself."

"Prepare myself for what?"

"For being traded or sent away," Ahune says. Then she leaves abruptly, before I can question her more.

I put the comb in my pouch and go in search of Jokul. The mamateek Jokul shares with Poorish's family is empty, but two children about eight years old are playing a game of sticks and stones in front of the opening. When I ask about Jokul's whereabouts, the older of the two points to the long beach behind the encampment.

"There," he says. "Where the whales come in."

I hurry to the long beach. Sure enough, at the far end I see a tall figure walking among the driftwood. Every so often, he stoops to pick up something. Jokul has his back to me so I'm able to get within speaking distance before he hears my footfall and turns.

"I want to talk to you about some news I've just heard."

Jokul sits on a log whose root looks like a horse's head.

"You mean the decision the old ones will be making

about us tomorrow?"

"Yes, if you think they're likely to kill us, I'd like to know so I can slip away tonight."

"They won't kill us. Our captors avoid killing others."

"They killed Grimkel."

"That was an exception."

"What will they do with us?"

"We might be traded. I might be traded to the Osweet, for instance, though I doubt it since I've made myself useful to Poorish and her children. They might trade you to the Owasposhno-un or the Washawet. Or they might send us away. I doubt they'll do any of those things." Jokul picks up the rib bone of a whale and turns it over.

"I would just as soon escape as be sent away," I say.

"Where would you go? It's not as if we know where we are."

"That's true, but if I followed the coastline North, I would eventually come to Leif's houses."

"But the houses will be empty. Everyone will be gone. I know Finnbogi Egilsson who owned the Icelanders' ship intended to stay in Leifsbudir only one year and your Greenlanders will have long since departed. What would you do there?"

"I'd wait."

"For what?"

"For a ship to rescue me."

"As far as I'm concerned, life's too short to wait for something that may never come. I'm thirty-one years old which means I've already lived more than half my life. You're younger by far. Maybe you've got time to wait for a ship. But you should bear in mind how few voyages are made to these parts. You know as well as I do that your people came here mainly to build yourselves a ship because ships are so scarce in Greenland. You remember the difficult crossing. Do you really think a ship can be risked to rescue you? Even if one eventually came here, you can't wait for it in Leifsbudir on your own. You'd be putting yourself in too much danger."

"I don't see the danger of waiting in Leifsbudir."

"Then you don't know about the Aswan."

"The seal people? There were no seal people in Leifsbudir."

"Not last year. But the Owasposhno-un tell me the Aswan have been seen there. Not often it's true. It depends on the supply of harbour seals. The Aswan aren't as peaceful as our captors. If they found you in Leifsbudir, they would kill you on the spot, since you are white."

"Why should my whiteness matter?"

"Because of what happened on this coast when Thorvald Eiriksson was over here. Surely you know the story."

Thorvald Eiriksson was Leif's younger brother. I was only four years old when Thorvald made a voyage to these parts, but like all Greenlanders, I remember being told the story of his death.

When I tell Jokul this, he says, "Think about it. Thorvald was killed because he and his men found nine Aswan on the shore sleeping peacefully under their skin boats. They slaughtered eight Aswan where they lay. The ninth one got away and told his people who came after the Greenlanders in a swarm of boats. Thorvald and his men managed to get away in their ship but not before Thorvald was killed by a wound in his throat."

"But that was far from Leifsbudir."

"Not so far for hunters like the Aswan who depend on harbour seals. The Owasposhno-un tell me the Osweet seldom go to Leifsbudir because they prefer to avoid the Aswan."

"Thorvald Eiriksson's death was ten years ago."

"That's not very long. It's within our lifetime and that of the Aswan. You can be sure that when the seal people gather around their fires at night, they tell the tale of how eight of them were slaughtered by white men while they slept."

I'm sure Jokul's exaggerating the situation, to keep me here. I tell him that I think it's strange that none of us saw the Aswan last year. "Leif Eiriksson never saw them either."

"You know his name, Leif the Lucky. The fact that he never met any of the people living here was nothing so much as chance. Leif was only here a year, and much of that time was spent exploring lands to the South. This country is so vast that people can avoid each other for long periods of time." Jokul picks up another whalebone rib and prepares to leave. "One last thing. Remember Grimkel. There are a few who would prefer to see us dead, not many, maybe one or two. It's safer if you stay with the Osweet old ones. They'll look after you. Don't try to escape. You'll only give someone who wants you dead a chance to hunt you down."

Jokul begins to walk away.

"Don't you miss Iceland?" I call after him.

He turns and says, "Not enough to return. My father was murdered in his bed to avenge a blood feud that was between our family and another for years. That's why I went to sea. I no longer have any desire to live among murderous Norsemen."

I sit on my rock and watch Jokul's body grow smaller and smaller then disappear behind a rise of ground. I know Jokul has an exaggerated view of Norsemen. Not all of them are murderous, my father for one. But it's certainly true that Norsemen are more vengeful than the Osweet.

For a long time I sit and stare at the sea shimmering in the sun. A light breeze lifts the water in such a way that it gathers small points of light everywhere. Far out, I see a whale's fin break the surface of the sea. I watch, waiting for the fin to reappear. I grow sleepier and sleepier. The warm sun makes my eyelids close and I fall, not into a dream but a memory. I remember, not the warmth of the Greenland sun which on a summer day fills the valleys with blinding light, but the bitter cold night in Winter when my family was nearly smoked out of our hut.

Erling and I were huddled together beneath a bearskin on the floor. Gunnhild was sleeping on one side of us, our parents and Magnus on the other. Mifelyn was sleeping on the other side of the hearth near the door. Sometimes the old woman kept me awake with her loud snores but not that night.

I was asleep but suddenly I wakened. In a darkness that smelled of smoke and fish, I heard something outside the hut. I lifted my head and listened. It sounded as though something large was being dragged in front of the door. There was a thumping sound. I crawled over Erling's sleeping form and shook my father awake. My father grunted his displeasure but he was willing to listen to what I had to say. He knew I would never have wakened him without good reason. I whispered into his ear.

My father sat up and listened. There was a scuffling sound on the roof. Then whale oil poured through the smoke hole and splattered onto the hearth. A burning rush was pushed through the hole and fell on the oil. Soon flames leapt up. My father grabbed a sheepskin and tried to beat out the fire. I shook my mother and the others awake.

"Help me with the door," my father said to my mother. He handed me the sheepskin. "Keep beating the fire."

My father and mother pushed against the door but it refused to budge.

More oil was poured from the roof. The flames leapt higher but I beat them down. Erling and Magnus began to scream. My father picked up the broad axe and chopped down the new door which had been made from wood obtained by trading our best milk cow.

I waited by the smoke hole, not close enough to have oil poured on my head, but close enough to put out the flames. But no more oil was poured inside. Instead, our neighbour Ketil Bjornsson screamed through the smoke hole, "Take heed, Ozur Einarsson, that your cattle do not stray into my home field again. I've had enough of your wayward cows. Keep them in your own field or next time you won't be as lucky as you are tonight!"

In the morning my father mended the door with scraps of driftwood, but it was never as tight as it had been before.

I see the whale's fin break the bright water close to shore. The whale's back curves into the sea, its glistening skin reflecting the sun. The sight of the whale reassures me. How pleasant to live side by side with whales, which seem to be the most carefree and generous of creatures. In Greenland we do not see whales often for our farm is inland, at the end of Einarsfjord, far from the sea. I think of the rib bones Jokul picked up from this beach and wonder if he has also become a carver.

18

The next morning, Imamasduit is nowhere to be seen. Bogodorasook rouses me from my bed, hands me a basket and tells me to wait by the canoes. The old ones will be meeting inside the mamateek, he says, and I must leave before they arrive. He says that if I'm hungry, I must find something to eat before I go since he and the other elders will be meeting on empty bellies. An empty belly, he tells me, sometimes makes a man's thoughts clear. I go outside with my basket, but not in search of food. There's a queasiness in my belly that began at dawn when I awoke with the reminder that my future and Jokul's will be decided today. I drink a cup of cold water and go to the canoes to wait. I am first to arrive.

A short distance to the North is a large island where eider ducks nest. I remember that when we paddled past the island on our way here, Bogodorasook mentioned we would be coming back soon to collect eider duck eggs. Everyone will be coming to the island. Only the old ones will be left behind. As I wait on the beach for the others, Abidith comes up to me. For once she's alone. Impulsively I reach into my pouch and take out the comb. I lift one of her hands and place the comb on its palm. Abidith stares at it in silence. I am also silent for I know the comb speaks my feelings better than any words could. Abidith rubs her fingers across the smoothness I worked so hard to achieve. Then she traces the outline of the ship. Finally she says, still looking at the comb, "It's a fine comb, Wobee, but I cannot accept it, for you have carved your dream into it and it is not the same as mine."

"It could be the same, in time."

Abidith lifts her eyes and stares at me.

"It will never be the same, Wobee, for I have already carved Watsut into my dream."

Abidith reaches for my hand and gently places the comb in it. Then she turns and walks toward her father and Watsut who are coming out of their mamateek.

I have the urge to throw the comb into the sea, but I can't bring myself to do that. Instead I return the comb to the pouch. At least Abidith did not toss the comb aside in anger as she would have once, which means she has some feelings toward me.

Dysee, Hathasut and their children arrive and I get into the canoe with them. Ahune has already seated herself at one end. I pick up a paddle and sit in front of her. From now on, I intend to use every opportunity that comes my way to improve my paddling. I am more determined than ever to escape, whether or not Abidith comes with me.

After we reach the island and beach the canoes, I take my basket and begin collecting eggs. The island is far from being steep but slopes up gently from the water, which means there are no cliffs to scale. Unlike most sea birds, eider ducks lay their eggs in low tufted places that are often marshy. I take off my shoes and tying them together, sling them over my shoulder, and roll up my breeches. As I trudge between nests, my feet sinking into the clumps of wet grass, the eider ducks flap and scold. Occasionally, a drake tries to nip my ankles but I kick it away. As I fill my basket, I think about taking one of the canoes and escaping. If I could manoeuvre a canoe to the other side of the island, I might be able to get far away without being seen. Then I remind myself that it would be foolish to take this risk. With several canoes close by, I would soon be caught. To escape my captors, I need a long head start without being seen. It's wiser to bide my time until I get a better chance.

Ahune comes up and peers into my basket. "I see your basket is half full, like mine."

"No, it's half empty like yours."

Ahune laughs. "Why don't we sit for a while in the sun?"

My feet are cold and wet from tramping through swamp. I welcome the chance to warm them. We find a large flat rock and sit down. Ahune offers me a raw egg but I refuse, and she eats it herself. Then she says, "You'll be pleased to know my sister Geijsuit has already agreed to be Zathrasook's wife."

"Why would I be pleased?" I say. "What difference does it make to me who Zathrasook marries?"

"Haven't you noticed how much more agreeable he is now that he's trying to impress Geijsuit?"

"I avoid Zathrasook," I say. "Because of what happened to Awadasut, Zathrasook despises me." Then I tell her about running down Awadasut.

Ahune frowns and says, "That's not the only reason Zathrasook despises you."

I turn sideways to look at Ahune. I think she might be playing a game with me, but it seems she's not. "Why else does he want me dead?"

Ahune returns my look. "Zathrasook doesn't wear a totem like other men."

For a long time I've known that Zathrasook doesn't wear the Osweet ornament around his neck. I don't know why I haven't asked Abidith or Imamasduit about this.

"The women tell me that you brought down the largest stag last year, a stag Zathrasook wanted so he could find his totem. Instead of giving the stag to him, the caribou spirit gave it to you."

"But I wear no totem."

"That's because when it was given to you, you didn't know what it was," Ahune says. "You weren't born under the Osweet sign. Sooner or later, everyone in our tribe wears the sign under which they were born. Whether it be a stag, a whale or a bear, for a man to earn his totem, he must kill an animal large enough to feed everyone in his family at the feast."

So this explains why Boasook and Hathasut wear a necklace of bear teeth while Tisewsut, Imamasduit and Thoowidith wear the sign of a whale's tail.

"How does a women find her totem?"

"It's different for a woman," Ahune says matter-of-factly. "A woman wears the family totem after she begins to bleed."

I turn away from Ahune, to hide my burning cheeks. She's wearing a necklace of bear teeth, which is the Washawet family totem.

"When a woman wears a totem, it's a sign she's ready to marry."

"Surely you're too young to marry," I say to tease her.

"I'm twelve," she says. "In two years I will choose a husband."

"The truth is I thought you were older," I say, looking steadfastly at the water. Were I to turn and look at her, I couldn't help looking at her womanly shape which might be interpreted as disrespectful.

She scowls. "That's because I'm bolder than other girls. I'm different from my sisters. I don't always like doing what other women do. Sometimes my father lets me hunt small game. My mother doesn't like me doing it, but I do it anyway. I would never choose to marry a man like Zathrasook who would order me about. Geijsuit does everything he says."

"You like your own way."

"Yes, but I would give my husband his."

Then she asks me to tell her about men and women in Greenland. I tell her that men own the farms which they give to their older sons.

"Are you an older son?"

"I have an older sister and two younger brothers." I tell her about them.

Ahune wants to know how someone can give away land. I explain about owning but it's hard for her to understand.

"Here the land belongs to the Creator," she says. "It's for his children's use."

"In Greenland a woman may own a piece of land she can walk around the edge of in a day while leading a cow."

When I explain what a cow is, Ahune laughs. "I've never heard of anything so strange. If I were to lead a caribou through the woods for a day, all I would have for my troubles would be sore feet and a scratched face."

We continue to trade stories long after the sun has warmed our feet. When the shadows of the rocks cast themselves on the beach, we resume our egg collecting. Some of the women are already waiting at the canoes for the rest of us to finish. Ahune and I fill our baskets in silence. I think that we've spoken so many of our thoughts that our heads are empty.

By the time we've paddled back to camp, the elders

are on the beach, waiting for us. We disembark and
the women feed the children a meal of fresh eggs and
roasted fish. Imamasduit appears, from nowhere it
seems. She takes my basket and sets the eggs to boil,
saying she'll grind them into a fine powder tomorrow.
I glance at Imamasduit, hoping she'll give me a sign
of what was decided by the old ones, but her face
gives nothing away.

19

Eventually when the children have been quieted and the camp-fire has settled into a bed of glowing coals, everyone gathers in a circle. There are many shufflings and whispers as people arrange and rearrange themselves. I stand on the edge of the circle, my belly tightening and cramping inside, acutely aware of my skin. I am the only one here who is white.

When everyone is silent, Bogodorasook takes the leg bone of a caribou from a pouch and holding it up, begins to speak. He has a strong voice, one that doesn't falter or shake.

"Since long before any of us was born, our people have been gathering here in the place where the Creator emerged from the sea. We've traded ochre, arrow stone, birch-bark, furs and bone. We've made marriages and alliances between our families. We've hunted and fished together. We've been through famine and plenty. By sharing in these ways, we've renewed and enriched the ties binding us together. Most years when we meet, the good times have been more plentiful than the bad. But bad things have happened. Some of our people have died from lack of food. Some of our women have been taken away by the Aswan. Some of our men have lost their scalps to hunters who have come across the water from the South. But these misfortunes have not happened often. For the most part we have been able to live well and in peace. Now a new danger has entered our lives. White men have appeared on our shore.

"The Creator put us in a big land where food is plentiful, but only if we move around. The seals are in one place, the salmon in another; the caribou wander where their spirit takes them. It's different from year to year. For our people to survive, we must go where the animals lead us. We must be free to travel our coasts. We cannot do this if white men obstruct us. Tisewsut will now tell us about the white men he saw last year on our northern coast."

Bogodorasook gives the caribou bone to Tisewsut. Tisewsut looks uncomfortable holding it. Maybe he's never spoken at a gathering before. When he begins to speak, his voice is weak but it gathers strength as he goes on.

"Late winter last year was bad for us. We had little food. Our people were hungry. The harbour seals didn't come to the nearby coves, and the winds kept the pack ice far from shore so we couldn't hunt the ice seals either. For this reason, six of us went as far North as we could go looking for seals. Only Shawbawsut had been that far North before. That was long, long ago, when he was young."

I don't think Tisewsut intends to tease but some of the women may think so for they laugh, thinking perhaps that Tisewsut jokes about Shawbawsut being older than he is.

"When we came out of the woods facing the bay, we saw there were white men living on the shore. They were big men with hairy faces and hair as yellow as summer flowers. The men had built themselves huge caves of earth and wood. On the shore were two large wooden tents which was where they kept their boats. Seeing all this from the woods, we decided we would not go any further, for there were many more white men than there were us. We also saw that we had arrived too late, that the wind had driven the pack ice beyond the open water which was too far for us to hunt seals. But there were many seal carcasses on the shore piled up around the caves. Shawbawsut said we should take one of the seals to strengthen us for our journey back to our camp. Because Awadasut was the fastest runner, he agreed to go. We made a night shelter further in the woods. Shawbawsut snared a ptarmigan and we roasted that. It was our first food in three days. Early the next morning, Awadasut and I returned to the shore for the seal."

As I listen to Tisewsut describe what happened that fateful morning, I hang my head with shame. None of the people look my way or give me the evil eye as they might have done under the same circumstances in Greenland.

"In order to have the strength to bring Awadasut back, Shawbawsut boiled his moccasins to make soup," Tisewsut says. "Before we reached our camp, the rest of us had done the same."

Tisewsut returns the leg bone to Bogodorasook who announces that Gwanesh of the Owasposhno-un will speak. Gwanesh stands up and, holding up a large piece of whale bone, begins to speak. His voice is as rough as coarse sand and as loud as thunder. He tells about the white men who four years ago came to the bay where the Owasposhno-un dig trenches to trap flounder. "The white men came in a huge canoe which had a tree in the middle. When the white men came ashore, the Owasposhno-un ran away and watched from the woods. The white men set up camp not far from the flounder traps. The next day at sunrise when the tide was out, Ashoo and Anuit crept out of the woods to empty the traps and the white men came after them with weapons. Shanduit and Poorish came out of the forest and showed their breasts. They beat upon them and shouted out that they were Ashoo and Anuit's wives, and that the white men should show their respect by leaving their husbands alone. But the white men ignored the women. They chased Ashoo and Anuit and cut them down like trees. If Shanduit and Poorish had not run off, they too might have been killed. No greetings or words of warning were exchanged. That is what white men did to my people."

Gwanesh sits down and Bogodorasook announces

that Ougen of the Washawet will speak. Ougen stands and, holding the skull of a bear in his hands, begins to speak. Ougen is a short, big chested man who looks much younger than either Bogodorasook or Gwanesh. He has a wide echoing voice that reminds me of a pebble being dropped into water. His words circle outward to surround our listening ears.

"The path of the Washawet hasn't yet crossed the white man's," he says, "but I have been considering the matter all day with my brothers. At first, when I heard two white men had been captured, I argued against keeping them since they are clearly inferior to us, for white men kill people without regard to who and where they are which makes them a brutal and savage enemy, one we are unable to respect. Why, I argued, should we keep company with warlike people when we want to live in peace? Why do these people come to our land when they have one of their own? Why don't they stay in their land? Why do they come to ours?"

Hearing these words, I feel I have swallowed a knife which is stabbing the inside of my belly. I'm sure I'm about to be cast out. I made a mistake. When I was on the island this afternoon instead of talking to Ahune, I should have risked an escape while I had the chance to use a canoe.

"But my brothers have pointed out that their captives have been good hunters and have helped make up for the loss of our men. Because our survival depends on having strong hunters, I have come to agree with the others that it would be unwise to send the white men away as long as they continue to work alongside us in peace. I have also been persuaded that these white men can be useful to us in other ways as well."

Hostages. I think he wants to keep Jokul and me to use as hostages against our people, should any of them return to these shores one day.

"If white men continue to come to our land, we should learn more about them. The better you know your enemy, the better you can defend yourself. We have decided to ask Cheething to tell us about his people and what we can expect from them."

Will I be asked to speak as well? Though I can understand most of what is being said, I'm less able to speak my thoughts. Jokul's more skilled in this regard, having lived with the Owasposhno-un for nearly two years.

Jokul gets up and begins to speak with empty hands. Compared to the other speakers, Jokul's voice is high; it goes up and down like a song. Because he's new to the language of red men, Jokul often gropes for words. But after a while, the words come together more quickly.

"I don't expect to see many white men coming here again. Norsemen live far from us and must journey many days across dangerous seas to get here. The Norsemen didn't come here to stay but to gather wood. They live on islands far to the North where there are no trees. And they need trees to build their ships.

"Norsemen are farmers who raise animals to feed and clothe themselves. They grow food as well. But they are greedy for goods. Even in countries where trees are plentiful, Norse farmers will go a-viking once their work is done. They take their ships to other countries to plunder and raid other farmers. They have long ships that can travel upriver and take unsuspecting folk by surprise. Norsemen have iron weapons and tools. It is these tools they use to build their large boats. Considering the size and speed of their boats and their iron weapons, it will be difficult to defend yourselves against them. What we have on our side is a knowledge of this country which the Norse do not have.

"My advice is to avoid Norsemen who come here for wood. They live a very different life from us. They divide up the land into fields and farms. They believe their reputation depends on how much they own. For that reason as well as others, even if a ship were here to take me back to Iceland, I would not go. The fact is I am far more content with you than I ever was with my people. I can tell you much more about Norsemen but it will take a long time and many years." Jokul pauses and looks at me. "Wobee can also tell you much. But we cannot tell you everything tonight. That is all I have to say for now except for one thing: not all Norsemen are murderers. Only some of them live the Viking way. Where I come from life is hard. Most Norsemen are too poor to own a ship and for that reason will never come here."

Jokul sits down and Bogodorasook stands up.

"Now we will hear from anyone else who wishes to speak."

One after the other, the men get up and speak. None of the women do. No one suggests that Jokul and I be cast out which surprises me. I had expected Zathrasook to urge the leaders to throw me out but he remains silent.

When the last of the speakers is done, Bogodorasook speaks again. He says that when all things are considered, there would be little point in casting Cheething and me out. "Cheething and Wobee are part of the exchange by which our people live: that we give and we take in the same amounts. Upsetting the balance goes against the harmony we seek. It is true that Cheething and Wobee were born white, but it may be that in time they will become red inside."

Those are the last words spoken around the fire that night.

People get up and move about. Mothers put their children to bed. A basket of boiled eggs is passed around. I take two, one for myself and one for Jokul. Jokul's sitting alone by the fire. Poorish has gone to her mamateek with her children.

"You spoke well, Jokul," I say in Norse. "I am sure our captors treated us more kindly as a result."

He looks at me as if I were a stranger. "My name is Cheething," he says in our captors' language. "Never call me by my former name. I am no longer the person I was."

I offer him an egg but he pushes my hand away. As I eat the eggs, I wonder how Cheething can be so sure that he is no longer the person called Jokul, since I know that although I am Wobee, I am also Thrand.

20

The next morning, Imamasduit tells me I am to be ochred today. She laughs. "No more white man," she says.

I am dismayed to learn that the women do the ochring, not the men. Fortunately, it's the older women who do this, not the young. I am shy about having Abidith see my nakedness, especially now that she knows how I feel about her.

Imamasduit tells me to stay inside the mamateek, to strip and lie belly down, in my sleeping place. After I've stretched out, Abidith's mother, Thoowidith, and Imamasduit grease my back. They rub the seal oil everywhere, in the crease of my behind, on the soles of my feet and on the palms of my hands. They work slowly, rubbing me so gently and firmly I nearly fall asleep. After the greasing, they rub red ochre into the grease and work it into my skin.

"Now you must lie on your back," Imamasduit says. She hands me a skin breech-clout. Neither she nor Thoowidith look away when I get up and put the breech-clout on.

I lie on my back and they grease my chest, thighs,

arms and legs, then ochre me all over, even inside my navel and ears.

They leave my hair until the end.

At last they finish. The ochring has taken a long time and I am hungry. When I tell Imamasduit this, she says, "No food until you're finished. Now you must ochre your sleeping skins and tools. If you were born one of our people, you would have had to fast for three days to prepare yourself for the ochring ceremony but since you were born white and are already a man, there has been no ceremony."

The women leave me alone with the baskets of ochre and grease.

While I'm reddening my things, I stop every so often to look at my red skin, to get used to it. At first, it merely looks coarse and gritty, somewhat like animal hide. It smells acrid and sharp. I think about the colour of human skin. Greenlanders' faces and hands are brown and rough from sun- and wind-burn, but the skin on the rest of their bodies is as soft and white as cheese. It also has the sour, pungent smell of cheese. I have never liked the white parts of my body. To me white is a feeble, weak colour, especially for a man. The colour is misleading, of course, for Greenlanders are far from being feeble or weak.

I look at my red skin with new eyes. I like the colour which is as much brown as it is red. I like its brightness which, with the grease beneath, seems to glow and pulse reminding me of the blood flowing through my limbs. Perhaps because I will it, the redness is already making me feel more vigorous and strong. It's as if I'm sheathed in a protective covering that will guard me from unwanted eyes, that as long as I'm wearing it, I will never be naked again. The more I think about being red, the more the redness appeals to me. Now I look more like the earth. I no longer seem as separate from the animals as I was, from the trees and plants that grow all around, from the streams and lakes whose water I drink. From now on I will feel more a part of them. When I first saw the Osweet, I thought the ochre was mainly used to protect the skin from sun and rain and biting insects. Though it will protect me in those and other ways, the ochre is already making me feel I am part of the land, even the forests I feared.

I am so caught up in these thoughts, I forget my hunger. At last I finish ochring my gear and go outside. The camp-site is empty. I see people among the rocks along the shore gathering shellfish. Everyone including children has a container of some kind and is gathering mussels and crabs. I pick up my basket and run to join the others, wading between the slippery rocks, looking for crabs before they scuttle into the seaweed and hide. When I reach into the water for a crab, I notice my fingers are still red. Because the ochre has been deeply worked into the skin, the redness doesn't come off in the water. How strange it is to see a red hand at the end of an arm that once was white.

21

Summer has arrived. The grass is green. In the woods birch and maple are leafing out. Buttercups and strawberry blossoms star the embankment above the shore. Angelica grows by the stream. Small silvery caplin come in with the tide and flap about on the shore. There are so many of these caplin that they make a foaming wave on the beach. The whales I've seen breaching and spouting in the bay follow the caplin in. Some of them come so close to shore, I can hear them breathe.

One morning, two of the Owasposhno-un canoes go out whale hunting. Ahune explains that the men will not be hunting the humpbacks or the giant fin whales. They will hunt a small whale they can manoeuvre with harpoons and canoes. Though these small whales are common to these waters, they are only hunted on special occasions.

"Even a small whale is big enough to feed us all at a feast," Ahune says. "As for the larger whales, every year at least one of them strands itself on the beach."

I know this already of course. Behind where Ahune and I are sitting on the long beach are the bones of countless whales that have come ashore. I shield my eyes against the sunlight and watch the men in the canoes. Far beyond them the black-and-white tails of humpbacks appear and disappear. Judging by the size of the tails, some of the whales are huge. With a flick of their tails, they could easily upset the canoes, which is why the hunters are careful about getting too close to the larger whales. It is easy to see why the Owasposhno-un have chosen a whale's tail as their totem.

"To find his totem, the hunter must be the one to land a harpoon," Ahune says. "Then the others will help tow the whale."

This is what happens, though it takes a long time. All morning Ahune and I sit on the beach, but the canoes move South of us and we do not see the harpoon being thrown. It isn't until afternoon that a small whale is towed in and the women fetch their tools to cut it up.

That night everyone gathers at the place of the stones where Fathoon of the Owasposhno-un performs a dance to the spirit of the whales. When she's finished, she gives everyone a piece of the boiled whale meat Gwanesh has cut, just as Imamasduit did at the caribou feast. Later Ahune tells me that since the death of Gwanesh's wife, his daughter Fathoon serves in her place. After everyone's been served, the basket of meat is passed around and the feast begins. As well as whale meat, there are strips of dried salmon, shellfish, and cakes made from berries and eggs. Bathsut, the young man who threw the harpoon, strides among the gathering, laughing and eating, knowing he has earned the right to wear the Owasposhno-un whale totem around his neck.

Fortunately the caplin run is strong and we are able to eat their roasted flesh as well as dry some for later on. As Ahune predicted, a humpback grounds itself on the long beach and we feast on it for many days. Then the salmon come and nets are set up in the bay facing our camp. Every day we get into canoes and empty them. The salmon also swim upstream. For a while so many salmon enter the stream beside our camp that it's an easy matter to wade into the water and pick them up. Any salmon that isn't immediately eaten is laid on a rack to dry.

   Lobsters and mussels are so plentiful they can be harvested without a canoe. There are so many lobsters that they are also dried on racks for later use. Several times we go hunting for sea birds on the islands. We also go into the woods to snare ptarmigan. The flounder come and we dig trenches for them. One day Shawbawsut and Tisewsut go into the woods and return with two beaver. With such an abundance of food, our bellies are never empty. We are lucky, for Ahune tells me that some years the summer gatherings have been cut short for lack of food. Now that the days are long, we often linger around the fire at night picking at morsels of leftover food. Although it's warm, a smudge fire burns all day and night to help keep the biting insects away. Here by the sea, the black flies are few since there's usually a breeze coming off the water, but occasionally when the breeze drops, the flies swarm in. When that happens, spruce boughs are laid on the fire and the smoke drives them away.

Cheething and I are helping Bogodorasook build a canoe. First we go into the birch grove with him to cut the bark, using the wood-handled knives the Osweet have made with stone knives. Choosing the biggest trees, Bogodorasook cuts large strips of birch-bark which we take back to the camp-site and carefully sew together with spruce roots to make one large piece. It's only when a canoe is being made that men cut birch-bark; otherwise the women harvest it.

One day when Bogodorasook has gone to look for more spruce root, leaving Cheething and me on the beach sewing birch-bark, Ahune wanders by.

"I'm pleased to see men doing women's work," she says. "For it makes it easier for women to do men's."

"So you want to be a man," Cheething counters, amused at her words.

"Sometimes. Men often get to do more interesting work whereas women are left with the dullest chores."

"Maybe they're dull because they're repeated so often," Cheething says.

Ahune sits on the grass, bends her knees and tucks her tunic beneath them.

"I'd like to learn how to build a canoe," she says.

"I'm learning myself," I tell her. "In Greenland we build prams."

I describe a pram: its keel, the boards we call strakes, the oars.

"They are rowboats," Cheething says. He explains how rowing is different from paddling. "They work well on the sea, but they wouldn't suit us here since they're too heavy to carry overland."

When Bogodorasook returns with the spruce root, he scolds Ahune, "Hasn't your mother work for you to do?"

After this, Ahune is careful to watch us only when Bogodorasook isn't there.

We finish sewing the birch-bark and set it aside. We go to the woods to find long spruce saplings which we shape into a frame for a keel and tie with roots. The large piece of birch-bark is laid on the ground and the keel centred on top. Very carefully the bark is folded over the frame and lashed. It takes many days to finish the keel, for the curved ends must be carefully pieced and sewn. When this has been done, the inside of the canoe is strengthened with crossbars and ribs made from specially shaped sticks. The top edges are fitted with a frame to protect them. When all this is done, the seams are covered with spruce gum and red ochre to make it waterproof. It takes us well over a month to make the canoe for we must stop often to fish and hunt. Making the canoe gives me so much pleasure that I often forget to mark each day on my calendar stick and I must guess how many grooves to cut.

Midsummer, on the day of the ochring ceremony, Cheething and I carry the new canoe and the paddles to the gathering place to be ochred but we aren't permitted to stay. Bogodorasook explains that we'll have to leave, that the ceremony is sacred to the red people but not yet to us. It is during the ceremony that new babies are reddened and named.

Cheething and I are walking along the driftwood beach where we've gone to get out of the way and to look for another rib bone. The bone is not for carving but for a building purpose. By stretching caribou skin over whale bones, he's making a smoke-house for meat and fish which he says will work better than outdoor racks. I ask Cheething if he believes the time will come when we'll be able to attend the ochring ceremony.

He shrugs. "I don't know but I hardly care. I've never been one for ceremonies. It doesn't matter to me whether I attend this one or not."

"We're expected to live like red men," I grumble. I am disappointed that I will not see Dysee's baby being named. "Yet we're treated like outsiders."

"In most respects, we're not treated like outsiders. You'd be more content if you remembered how much these people share with us."

I try to follow Cheething's advice for I know what he says is true, that we live among people who share. The rest of the Summer we are included in everything else. The warm days slip by with everyone mingling together. Our bodies grow sleek and plump from the abundance of food. It requires so little effort to feed ourselves that after the basic chores are finished, we have plenty of time to rest. Sometimes I lie in the shallows of the water and let the waves wash over me. Afterwards, when the sea dries on my skin I see that my arms and legs are still red from the ochre and grease that have been rubbed deep into me. Even so, I apply another coating of ochre and grease to my hands. Often when I'm sitting by myself, someone from the Owasposhno-un or the Washawet families will come and speak with me. Usually it's Ahune. Zathrasook never speaks to me, but neither does he throw hostile looks my way as he once did. It may be, as Ahune says, that her sister has made Zathrasook more agreeable. Certainly Ahune has made me more content. One way and another, she's added to the pleasure of Summer.

22

Grandmother and I are on the shore in the place of stones. This is a stretch of shoreline beyond the plateau that people pass on their way to the driftwood beach. Here the Creator has arranged large smooth stones in such a way as to provide enough sitting places for all of us in the flat openess. This was the space where Fathoon performed the dance to the whale spirit several days ago.

Whenever I come to this place—and I have come here with Watsut often this summer—I imagine myself dancing, my head tilted back, my arms spread wide as I open myself to both the visible and invisible world.

I know Grandmother has asked me here to talk one last time about my decision to marry Watsut, for after our gathering disperses, which will be soon, it will be too late for me to have second thoughts.

After we have found ourselves sitting places on the sun-warmed rocks, Grandmother says, "Watsut is a fine young man. He will make a good husband. But by marrying him, you will have to leave the Osweet in two years to live with the Owasposhno-un, whereas if you marry Koorsook, the Washawet would agree to let him live with us. Ougen approached me one day and told me this. He thought you might be persuaded to choose Koorsook."

"Grandmother, I have thought about marrying Koorsook," I say carefully, "but I prefer to marry the man I like best, even though it means living apart from my family."

Grandmother is silent for so long that I think she must be displeased with me. Finally she lifts her face toward the sun and says, "You are doing what your mother and grandmother have done."

More than once during the gathering I have asked myself if I was choosing Watsut because my mother and grandmother were born Owasposhno-un. I wondered if I wanted to marry back into their family. Watsut and I have talked about this.

"Maybe the Owasposhno-un are getting back something they lost when you and my mother came to live with us," I tell Grandmother, repeating one of Watsut's jokes.

Grandmother doesn't laugh. "I remember it being a difficult choice for me to make. It was a difficult choice for your mother also. But we knew in time that we would become the place and the people where we live."

"We become part of each other," I say. This is something I have not spoken aloud before though I know it to be true. Sometimes I feel so close to Grandmother, to my mother and sister that I feel I am carrying them inside. I can see their tiny bodies inside mine, sleeping like babies.

"It is difficult," Grandmother goes on, "but eventually we can become part of another place. The trees, rocks and streams of a new place slowly enter us. Our red world is large enough to enclose us all." She reaches out and strokes my hair. "When you leave us to live with Watsut, you will still be inside your mother just as she is inside me and I am inside my mother and she is inside her mother."

I remember being inside my mother. For me, memory and thought are one and the same. I close my eyes. I see myself inside my mother's belly, cradled in a small red sea. Even then I knew the world outside my mother's belly was red. All our people are born knowing this. They are also born knowing the spirit world is red and that they are joined to it, joined to those who are sleeping as well as those who are not yet born.

I see my brother sleeping peacefully in his grave on the island, enclosed by red stones. For the first time since his death, I can think of Awadasut more with gratitude than grief. What a kind brother he was, gentle and patient, ready to understand. I know he would be pleased to know I have chosen Watsut for my husband.

I tell Grandmother about Wobee's comb, that I could not take his gift because Watsut was inside my dream. It is not the Osweet custom to return a gift, but neither could I take Wobee's dream.

"But you could take the eating tool Wobee made for Dysee's son," Grandmother says, sly as ever. "Now that Mandshet is named, there is no reason why he cannot have the tool."

I laugh and hold my grandmother close. How good it is to be free of the bitterness I once felt toward Wobee.

Grandmother and I rock together. Then she says so softly the stones cannot hear, "You will make a good dancer." She gives me a slight push. "Dance for me."

I get to my feet and there in the flat openness, I tilt my head back so far my hair hangs down like a waterfall. Then lifting my arms toward the sky, I will my body to carve the air, to shape its invisibility and light, to make it the story of our being. I dance for Grandmother, for Grandfather and all the Osweet. I dance for my brother and all those who are in the spirit world. I dance for the Washawet and the Owasposhno-un. I dance for the unborn, not only Watsut's children who I will one day carry inside, but all those who will walk on this beach one day. I dance for the spirit of the caribou, the bear, the whale and the other animals who are part of our dream. I dance for our redness, for the blood that flows through us all. Not the blood of killings and murder but the blood of harmony and peace. I dance for Wobee. As I dance, carving the light with the shape of my moving self, I become as joyful as a bird or a whale. I become the dream, flowing, shaping, changing, moving with the sun and moon.

Six

23

Summer has begun to wane which means I have been with the Osweet a year. The shadows now appear longer than the trees and the breeze, though mild, is brisk. It's no longer warm enough to go without tunic and breeches. The strawberries have been eaten and the blueberries are now ripe and plentiful enough to fill our baskets many times over. Everyone, even the smallest children, go berrying. After they are picked, most of the berries are mixed with seal oil and stored in pouches for winter use. Once all the berries are harvested, we will return to our winter camps, for the season of caplin and salmon is over and we are eating dried fish and what beaver can be hunted, which isn't enough to feed us all.

The evening before we leave, two marriages take place at the same time. Cheething and I stand with the others to watch the ceremony which ends with long speeches given by the new wives' fathers. When the last of the speeches is over, a circle dance begins. The newly married couples join hands and dance around the fire. After they've circled the fire once, they drop hands and take others into the dance, making a new circle around the fire. Over and over they do this until all of us, including Cheething and me, are dancing. Round and round we go, faster and faster, until breathless and laughing, we drop our hands. Later that night, we feast on cakes made from dried lobster and egg which are smothered with mashed blueberries.

The next morning, we take down our mamateeks and carry them to the canoes. We gather our supply of ochre and arrow stone, enough to last us until the next gathering. These exchanges were made earlier. Each family brought their goods to the shore and laid them out so that everyone could see what there was. Nothing was hidden away or withheld. The Owasposhno-un laid out their ochre and birch-bark. The Washawet laid out their arrow stone and white bear furs. The Osweet laid out caribou skins and black bear furs. I felt pride laying out the walrus rope for it seemed to me the Osweet were at a slight disadvantage in the tribe when it came to trade. Except for the walrus rope, we had offered nothing that the others did not have. The exchange of goods was quietly done without any argument or hard words. The leaders trusted each other to be fair. This was so different from watching Greenlanders barter with Norwegian and Icelandic traders. Few ships come to Greenland and when they do they bring damaged goods: dented cups, tarnished brooches and planks pitted with termite holes. Greenlanders know they are at a disadvantage and haggle in an effort to get more for their goods. Often a fight breaks out when a farmer's wife parts with more of her cheese and wadmal than she thinks fair.

The food we'll be carrying with us is mainly intended for winter use. As for our meals during the journey, we'll harvest what there is on the way. As long as fish and small game are plentiful, we'll have enough to eat.

It is difficult for me to leave Cheething. Although he has been reluctant to talk about his past and has often avoided me, he is a connection with my previous life that I don't want to sever. We don't say goodbye. None of the people do. Abidith does not even speak to Watsut but gets into the canoe with the rest of us and does not look back as we paddle away.

We travel North, past the island where we harvested eider duck eggs. I'm paddling the new canoe with Bogodorasook. We'll be travelling with the Washawet until they come to the place where they turn West.

That night we camp with the Washawet sharing a circle of fire-blackened stones on the southern side of the promontory on whose northern side we camped on our way here. Bogodorasook makes a fire using the fire stone he carries in his pouch. After we've made camp and eaten, Ahune and I walk along the shore away from the others.

"I've something to tell you, Wobee, before we part. Some of the young women mistrust you. They think you don't know who or what you are," Ahune begins.

"Why should I care what they think?"

"I don't mistrust you," Ahune continues. "I like what you are."

"How do you know what I am," I say roughly, "when I don't know myself?"

"*I* know."

"You think you do."

"It's foolish to talk like this," Ahune says. "What does it matter?"

"It matters to me who I am."

"Then you must do something about it, and soon," Ahune says briskly. "I don't intend to wait forever to marry you."

I'm so astonished by this forthright declaration that I can think of nothing to say.

Ahune puts something in my hand. It feels cool and hard. I look down and see a round white stone glowing in the dusk.

"It's a Creator's stone. Carrying it will keep you safe," she says and walks quickly away.

For a long time I sit on the beach, my hand holding the white stone, looking at the still water which becomes blue-black in the darkening night. This is the last night I will see Ahune. Earlier, I heard Ougen tell Bogodorasook that because we made such good time today, the Washawet should be able to reach the narrows tomorrow. They will camp there and cross to their land in the morning while the fine weather holds.

Bogodorasook said the Osweet will follow the coast only as far as the place where we carry the canoes overland to the lakes.

I think about Ahune's declaration that she would marry me. I smile at her forthrightness, at her willingness to challenge me. As a companion, Ahune would never be dull, she would always be surprising me. I think about Cheething's advice to give up all thought of returning to Greenland. It's probably true, as he says, that the ships will be gone, that none will return for me. But how can I be sure? Probably it's also true that in many ways living among red people would be better than living among Norsemen. I think I could remain here and in most ways be content. Gradually I would become less of a white man and more of a red man. In time I might learn who I am.

But my family in Greenland wouldn't know this. They would worry and wonder and doubtless think me dead. This is what troubles me most. This is why I think I should return to Leifsbudir. As long as there's even the slightest chance a ship might be there, I must try to reach my parents, Gunnhild and my brothers, or at the very least, send a message to them.

Ougen told Bogodorasook that the Washawet will leave at dawn, before the rest of us stir. The Osweet will sleep late for they have only a short distance to go along the coast before they reach the camp where they'll turn inland, following the route which brought us to this coast, until they reach the camp where we spent the Winter. Some of their supplies will be left there as they continue on to the bay where I was staked a year ago. I heard Bogodorasook tell Ougen that the Osweet will camp beside the eastern bay as long as fish are plentiful. He also said they would hunt black bears which will now be fat from eating berries.

My intention is to camp with the Osweet tomorrow night. Then while they sleep, I will make my escape, using a canoe to follow the coastline North. By getting an early start, I can put myself far enough ahead that no one will catch me. It will depend on how hard I can paddle. If I can stay ahead of the Osweet, I should make it to Leifsbudir in three or four days. The coastline I'll be travelling will be new to me, but I remember Thorvard describing it once. I know it continues North before it turns East and crosses a wide bay. I remember Thorvard saying that the northern coast is long and low which means I'll be able to go ashore anywhere I choose.

The next day, as I paddle North with Bogodorasook and the others, I wrestle with my decision to leave. Maybe I should tell Bogodorasook my intention. He's never shown me anything but kindness and has helped me in countless ways. He might even help me if he knew I wanted to return to Leifsbudir. He might offer me the use of the canoe he and I built with Cheething. I decide to tell him my plans. Then I realize that I can't tell him, for if there's a ship in Leifsbudir, I will never return to the Osweet.

I know it won't be Freydis and Thorvard's ship for it was their intention to leave Leifsbudir last Summer. The Icelander Finnbogi Egilsson will also be gone. But Jokul told me Finnbogi's brother Helgi intended to stay in these parts for more than a year if it suited him. I know that Helgi travelled South with the Norwegian shipbuilder looking for oak wood. If Helgi built the ship he wanted, he might have decided to stay on in Leifsbudir for a time. If he's there, I'll join his crew, if he'll take me on. Though I'm not an Icelander, considering my circumstances, he wouldn't refuse.

Although I can't tell Bogodorasook my intention to leave the Osweet, I decide that once I have arrived safely in Leifsbudir, I will haul the canoe onto land and cover it with spruce boughs to protect it from winter snow. The Osweet aren't likely to travel that way soon, but if they do one day, they will find the canoe. In that way, they'll know I didn't regard taking the canoe lightly.

That night as we are eating, I see Abidith take the spoon I carved for Mandshet out of a bundle and give it to him. I watch as he grasps the handle and hits the spoon against the bowl in his mother's lap. Liking the sound it makes, he does it again and again. Watching the baby hold something I made affects me in such a way that I cannot look at him without regretting my decision to leave. After the meal is finished, I leave the circle for I prefer to avoid Bogodorasook and

Imamasduit, and Abidith, who must not guess my thoughts. The truth is I can't look any of the Osweet in the face. They have been kind to me yet I am about to take their new canoe, a canoe that is needed to carry goods. Going without the canoe will make life harder for them. There's no use trying to persuade myself that because I helped make the canoe it's partly mine, for I know that the canoe doesn't belong to anyone in particular but to everyone. To make my betrayal worse, Zathrasook finally acknowledges me. He sees me brooding by myself away from the others and beckons me to join Tisewsut and him by the campfire. I do so, but only to avoid arousing suspicion. Ahune is right. Her sister seems to have made Zathrasook more content. He seems to have set aside the idea of killing me, for the time being at least.

That night I have a terrible dream. My father is going from farm to farm in Greenland, trying to exchange the posts and beams he brought from Leifsbudir for a cow. It seems he did not build my mother a house after all. When he returned to Gardar without me, he found that during our absence our family had fallen on hard times. The cattle had died of cow fever the previous Winter and there was a scarcity of food. Mifelyn died in late Winter and Glub ran off, which made life hard for my mother. Now my father must trade the posts and beams for some food. No one will trade with him. It has been a hard Winter in Gardar and people are short of food. My father plods from farm to farm. He passes Sigurd Arnesson's farm. He knows Sigurd died a few days earlier and that his cow is going unmilked. My father decides to take the cow home and milk it until Sigurd's kin claim it as theirs. He would be doing them a favour by looking after the cow. My father finds a length of rope inside Sigurd's dairy hut. He loops it around the cow's neck and leads her toward the gate. He gets as far as the path before the door of Sigurd's hut opens and a young man my father doesn't know bursts outside brandishing an axe. The man comes after my father, intent on killing him. I try to move my legs to run to my father's side but my legs won't move. I groan and thrash about in my sleep until I wake.

After this I am afraid to sleep but lie awake some distance from the others, staring up into the clear sky, trying to locate the star sculptures my father showed me when I was a boy. Because of the lightness of the summer sky in Greenland, it's difficult to see the stars at this time of year. But during the Winter, my father often showed me the stars over our hut in Gardar. There is no doubt that tonight's dream is an omen, a warning to carry through with my escape. For if there is any chance of returning to Greenland, I must try to go home. My family is in trouble and needs my help. I am convinced that without me there to do my share of the work, my family is suffering. I owe it to them to put all my efforts into returning home as soon as I possible so I can help them.

Finally, when the last log crumbles into coals and flakes of ash, I get up and go to the canoe. Once I couldn't have walked so softly; I didn't know how. Now I am leaving the people who taught me this. I lift the canoe and carry it to the water. Carefully, I set rocks inside for ballast. I take no food, no weapons, only the skin pouch containing two wooden hooks I have made, my tools and carvings, and Ahune's white stone. There's nothing inside the canoe but a fishing line and two paddles. I pick up a paddle and, bracing its tip against the sea bottom, push myself quietly away from shore.

24

I am not a good paddler. I am strong enough but my movements are clumsy instead of smooth. Often I chop the water instead of pushing it back. Even so, with a steady arm and an empty canoe, I make good progress. I don't stop on any of the islands but continue paddling all morning without a break. By the time the sun is overhead, I have reached the place where the water narrows and the outline of Ahune's land takes shape on the opposite shore. If the Washawet followed their plan, they began their crossing early this morning and by now will be near the other side. I can't see them, of course. Though their land is close, it's not so close that I can see people on their shore from here.

I slow down, looking for a suitable place to go ashore and rest. I am being cautious in the event that for some reason the Washawet are still on this side of the water. If they haven't made the crossing and are on this coast, I want to see them first, to give myself time to hide. They would be suspicious of me travelling alone.

I come to a wide inlet with rock arms on either

side. I notice a stream flowing into the sea where one of the arms joins a shoulder of land. As I approach the stream, I see a circle of fire-blackened stones close by. The camp is empty. I go ashore and drink some water and take a brief rest. The fire ring is warm, warmer than the sun would make it. The warmed stones tell me the Washawet have recently left. Relieved, I allow my body to relax. Pleasant though it is, I don't linger here. Beside the stream are grassy meadows blue with berries. I pick a handful of berries and continue on.

The shore continues in small inlets and coves. I stay close to shore to avoid the pull of the northern current flowing South. I also want to be close to land in case strangers appear. But I see no one. In fact I see nothing living except two harbour seals.

By early evening, I reach a stretch of shore which has no inlets or bays. As Thorvard said, the land here is low. The shoreline is nothing but flat rocks sloping gently into the water. By now I am exhausted. I can scarcely lift my arms to paddle. But I don't stop. I continue dipping my paddle into the water though my movements have become sluggish and weak. Finally I come to a small cove where a narrow stream trickles onto the shore. There are no trees or shelter of any kind, but I am too weary to care. I haul the canoe ashore, drink some water and fall exhausted on the grass.

I waken with the sun shining on my face. It's long past sunrise. I am ravenous but I don't want to take the time to fish. I drink more water, eat more blueberries, not bothering to sort out the leaves, stuffing one handful after another into my mouth, and continue on. Now the shoreline turns steadily East. I know I am approaching the place where the land ends. Despite my hunger, I am feeling energetic and strong. I paddle until mid-afternoon without going ashore, working my way steadily along the coast until I come to the place where the land ends in a cape. Still I continue on. I must be sure that the cape is in fact where the land ends. When at last I round the cape, I am rewarded by the sight of a large island far away in the distant haze. I know that island. I have seen it before. It is one of two islands at the mouth of the bay where Leif built his houses. Another day and I will be there!

Exhilarated by this discovery, I paddle along the eastern shore of the cape and into a small bay. Here I drop a line in the water, using a wooden hook. Immediately, there's a strike and I haul in a large sea trout, coiling and flapping at the end of the spruce root. I am so hungry I sink my teeth into the flesh and eat it raw. Even if I were on land, I wouldn't be able to cook the fish since I do not have the reddish brown stone the Osweet use to make a fire. Despite my hunger, I can only eat half the fish. I set the rest aside for later and paddle ashore. There's still some daylight left and after the canoe has been hauled onto the shore and I've found a stream of water, I walk along the beach and climb the promontory at the end. From here I can look across a wide bay to another headland. Now I can see the smaller of the two islands facing Leifsbudir. A half-day's journey and I'll be at Leif's houses. I want to lift my arms and shout, but I've learned the hard way how to be prudent. Instead I return to the canoe, get inside and go quietly to sleep.

Early the next morning, I cross the bay, climb the second headland and for the first time in a year, get a glimpse of the cove facing Leifsbudir. The water in front of the houses is empty. There is no ship. Not even a pram breaks the surface, only a few rocks sticking up here and there. Though I was half expecting it, exhaustion and hunger have left me unable to accept this outcome and I slump to my knees. For a long time, I lie and weep. Since my capture, at the back of my thoughts there has always been the hope that I will one day be reunited with my family in Gardar. That hope has finally been smashed. It reminds me of my mother's earthenware bowl which I broke as a child. My father had paid a trader three sheepskins for the bowl which my mother treasured above anything else we owned. After I knocked the bowl off a bench and smashed it to pieces, my mother tried to stick the pieces back together with mud. It was a futile task. In the end she threw the bits and pieces into the trash. What I must do with my hope is to find a way of mending it. I know that in so doing I will have to throw some of it away. I have been depending too much on chance, willing myself to change circumstances far beyond my power. It is hard for me to accept what I cannot change for I am someone who must prove everything for himself. This is why I couldn't take Cheething's advice regarding the ship. I had to find out for myself that it wasn't here. Even though I know this to be true about myself, so stubborn is my hope, so tenacious are my dreams that when I return to the canoe and fall asleep, the vision of a ship awaits.

I see it clearly. It's the Icelanders' ship. It's not in front of the houses because it's under repair. On the way back from Vinland, the ship ran aground on some rocks and damaged the strakes. After many difficulties, Helgi Egilsson manoeuvred the ship back to Leifsbudir and brought it into the ship cove to the South of the houses. Now the Norwegian shipbuilder and his men are at work shaping new boards to replace the broken strakes. As soon as they are finished—and it will be any day now—they will bring the repaired ship into the bay and anchor it in front of Leif's houses for loading. Then they'll be ready for their journey home.

I awake feeling better for I have again convinced myself that the Icelanders are here. I saw them in my dream. Their ship isn't anchored in front of the houses. That's why it can't be seen from here. The ship is under repair in the cove beyond the meadow. I hurry back to my canoe and paddle around the headland

and along the other side. I'm still too far from the houses to see any of the Icelanders. Because of the lay of the land, the many inlets and coves, not to mention small islands, the sightline between Leifsbudir and myself is blocked. I paddle straight across the water to a small promontory. This outcropping is narrow and curves around the beach on one side of Leifsbudir. For some reason—it must be caution—I climb the rocks to take a closer look at the houses. This saves my life.

Pulled up on the beach ahead of me are four skin boats which I didn't see before. Maybe I was too far away to see them, or maybe they weren't there when I looked. I see two men outside the houses. One of them is facing my direction! This is all I see before ducking down. Did he see me? I wait, listening for a shout. I hear nothing but the sea lapping against the shore. I crawl sideways until I come to a rock that rears up higher than the rest. I crouch behind it and peer around to get a second look at Leifsbudir. Both men now have their backs to me. As I watch, two more men come around the houses. They are short in stature with glossy black hair. I think of the seal-hunting skraelings Greenlanders have described seeing in Northsetur. Like them, these men are dressed in sealskin tunics. The Aswan Cheething spoke about.

I scan the shore looking for signs that will tell me more. Then I see them: harbour seals are all over the rocks to the East of the houses. This is why the Aswan have come. No doubt they would have come before had these seals been here, but during our year in Leifsbudir, the only harbour seals we saw were one or two which surfaced briefly in the bay then disappeared.

I return to the canoe and force myself to think clearly about my situation. The Icelanders aren't here. If they were, they would be living in the houses. There is nothing here but memories and dreams. What I imagined in my sleep was a trick of my mind. There is no chance of my getting back to Greenland, not even a chance of sending a message by way of the Icelanders to my family, telling them that I am alive. The dream of my father that terrified me three nights ago is probably not true, any more than last night's dream of the Icelandic ship is true. Dreams live in a country of the mind where the real is interchangeable with the unreal. Perhaps it isn't a country at all, for dreams have no boundaries but move across water and land as if there were no space between. They move through time in much the same way, as if nothing separates the present from the past. Last year is never tarnished, but shines as brightly as today. What kind of dreams will mend my hope?

The Osweet could help me dream but only if I return to them, not as a captive but as someone who wants to become part of their lives. The Osweet might not be pleased to see me again, for in their eyes I had ceased to be a captive and was slowly becoming one of them. They are bound to be confused about why I wanted to escape. Of course I did not know then what I know now, which is that I have been more a captive of the past than I have been of the Osweet. By running away, by choosing to return to Leifsbudir, I turned my back on their willingness to let me enter their red world. They gave me something I would not accept. Remembering how disappointed I was when Abidith refused my gift of a comb, I know I must expect the Osweet to be disappointed in me, for not only did I refuse their gift, I took the canoe I helped build. That was a betrayal of their trust. Before I can expect to be accepted again, I will have to find a way of earning back that trust.

There are two ways of returning to the Osweet. I could go back the way I came which would mean carrying the canoe overland to the lakes and following the river to the winter encampment, and from there to the coastal camp. This would take seven or eight days, twice the time I spent getting here. Or I could continue East then follow the coast South until I come to last summer's camp. This I could do in two or three days. I might even get there before the Osweet. The thought of being there when they arrive pleases me. I imagine the new canoe drawn up on shore, a supply of firewood laid by, freshly caught fish drying on the racks. The prospect of welcoming the Osweet to their camp shines so brightly I decide to take the faster route.

The difficulty with this route is that I will have to

cross the bay in front of the houses. I cannot risk this in daytime, of course. I will have to do it at night. If the Aswan see me, the likelihood is that they will hunt me down. Bogodorasook says the Aswan are fierce. It is certain they would kill me for right away they would see my blue eyes and would realize that under my ochre covering I am white. As Cheething said they would remember the tale of Thorvald Eiriksson and his crew slaughtering eight of their men.

The promontory ends in a deep inlet. The inlet is where I'll wait until dark. The surrounding hills are bare except for grasses and low bushes. Thick alders grow along the shore. I paddle to the end of the inlet and pull the canoe into the alders. I doubt the Aswan will come this way, but if they do, the canoe will be concealed from them. I'm hungry. The only food I've had all day was the last of the fish which I ate this morning. There are blueberries growing on the slope and I forage for these before I crawl into the canoe and stretch out beneath the screen of green leaves. Though not for long. Soon I creep out of my hiding place and scour the shore until I find a smooth, flat rock that will suit my purpose. I take the rock back to the shelter, and with my knife, carve the runes which say THRAND OZURSSON LIVED HERE. When I finish the last of the runes, I lay the rock on the bottom of the canoe.

25

For a while, I sleep. When I waken, the night is far gone. I get up quickly and put the canoe in the water. There is no moon but there are plenty of stars. The moonless night provides the darkness I need for cover. But it means I must paddle farther out than I would if there was moonlight. I remember there are many rocks in this bay that must be avoided. I must also avoid the seals. If I come too close to them, they will bawl their alarm. Are the Aswan sleeping inside the houses? If they did, they wouldn't hear the commotion through the turf walls. But the Aswan mightn't be used to turf houses and may choose to sleep outside. If that is so, they'll hear the bawling and wonder what's disturbing the seals. The wind is blowing off shore bringing with it the fishy odour of seal carcasses.

I make a wide enough arc around the rocks to avoid disturbing the seals. I can smell them too. There's just enough light to see the outline of a small headland to the South. On the other side of the headland is the ship cove. I make for there. By this time, darkness is beginning to fade. I go ashore and walk along the beach until I find a log I know is there above the tide line. I used to sit on this log and watch the shipbuilders work. Even now, the smell of spruce chips lingers in the air. I scoop out a wide shallow hole in the coarse sand, in the protection of the log. I lay my rune stone in the hollow, and using some nearby stones, build a small mound over it. Now I am ready to continue South.

I get into the canoe, but I have only taken a few strokes before I turn back. It's still dark enough for me to creep across the meadow and take one of the Aswan's seals. I don't have the tools to slaughter a live seal, but I can take a carcass instead. All I have to do is bring it across the meadow on foot and put it into the canoe. How pleased the Osweet will be to have fresh seal. I imagine all of us feasting on the meat. I am sure the Osweet will understand that the seal meat is my attempt to return the seal Awadasut tried to carry back.

Taking the seal will be risky, but now that the idea of returning with it is firmly in mind, I am unwilling to give it up. It's a challenge I have set myself that's in some way connected to the kind of person I hope to become.

As a precaution, I hide the canoe beneath the alders on the shore of the ship cove and take the path through the woods. This is a short cut to the meadow behind the houses. When I lived in Leifsbudir, I walked this path many times. I smile to myself as I think how frightened I was then of the forest, believ-

ing as many Greenlanders do, that monsters and trolls
lived there. As a red man, I have become so accustomed to the woods that even in the half-dark I am
unafraid. I think of the dreams I had of forest giants
in which the trees took on the shape of my fears.
Those dreams stopped after I was ochred, for once I
had been reddened with earth, I felt I was no longer
separate from the forest, but part of it. Now I can pass
through darkened woods without fearing the trees.

But I am afraid when I come to the meadow. Though
the air is grey, the meadow is open. There is no cover of
any kind. If one of the Aswan looks my way, he would
see a human shape moving toward him across the
meadow. That is a chance I will have to take. I reach
the houses and take cover behind the shed where
Freydis Eiriksdottir used to store our food under lock
and key. The breeze has shifted to the East and the
strong odour of the seal meat wafts my way. The smell
is coming from the direction of the stream.

The stream is hard by the end house. Sure enough,
when I reach the end house, I see a pile of gutted
seals. Skinned seal is slippery to hold. I hook my fingers into a mouth and drag the carcass across the
meadow. I move backwards, keeping my eyes on the
houses. Then I see the shapes on the ground. As I
feared, the Aswan are sleeping outside the houses!

No sooner do I realize this than one of the hunters
stirs. As I watch he gets up and walks a short distance
from the sleeping bodies in order to relieve himself. At

first, he doesn't see me. I stand still, knowing any movement will attract his eye. In spite of my motion-lessness, as he returns to the others, he sees me. I hoist the carcass to my shoulder and begin to run.

I run across the meadow, carrying the carcass of the seal. The seal is heavy and slides off my shoulder so that I must stop and shift it over and over again. In some places the meadow is thickly grown with osier and bog laurel. I avoid these, choosing to run over moss and lowbush blueberries instead. I hear shouts behind me. I glance over my shoulder and see four Aswan coming behind. They are shorter than me but powerfully built. With my longer legs I am a faster runner. But I am slowed down with the weight and the slipperiness of the seal.

I keep on, occasionally stumbling over clumps of grass. The shouts grow louder. Now when I glance behind, I see that one of the Aswan is gaining on me. He's carrying a harpoon. I drop the seal but it's too late. The harpoon has already been thrown. It slices my right arm, on the side, below the shoulder. I lift my left hand and feel the warm stickiness of my blood. Cradling my wounded arm, I run faster and faster. My legs carry me far ahead. But I'm nowhere near the path that would take me to the canoe hidden in the ship cove. I must have cover. If I keep losing blood, I'll begin to lose speed. I must have a place to hide. My red body crashes into the bushes and I disappear into the trees.

26

I am lost. For days I have been wandering through the woods, foraging for berries and sleeping beneath the trees. I often see fresh bear scat but have yet to see a bear. Because of the bear signs, I think I may be nearing the place where I was abducted last year. But nothing looks familiar, or maybe it is that everything looks familiar. I keep circling back on myself. If I were to walk East in a straight line, I would eventually come to the sea. Then I could find some kelp and pound it with a rock until its juice ran free. I could find some ashes from an old camp-site to mix with the kelp juice to make a paste that would help my wound. If I were beside the sea, I would know where I was. I could follow the coastline South until I came to last summer's camp. By now the Osweet will be there. But I dare not risk going to the sea since the Aswan might be on the coast. I have been in the woods so long, I doubt they would be looking for me, but they might be hunting harbour seals along the shore. For the same reason there's no question of returning to the ship cove for the canoe, even if I could find my way there.

Many days and nights pass and I am still no closer to knowing where I am. Each day I am weaker and more confused than I was the day before. The wound is gradually weakening me. It feels rough and jagged to the touch, the area around it sore and red. My body is swollen from insects which have bitten through ochre and grease. Everywhere there are bright red needle pricks where flies have tasted my blood. The lack of food is also slowing me down. I cannot walk far without stopping often. One day I find a sharp rock and dig up a spruce root to make a snare, hoping to kill a ptarmigan. So far I have had no luck. Whenever I come upon a lake—it's always the same lake—I peer into it looking for fish, but the water is empty. I know that as long as I circle the lake, I will have drinking water. But I cannot stay near this lake forever. Without weapons and tools or warm clothing, I would never survive the Winter. Already it's cool at night, though not cold enough to kill the flies.

One day I snare a small bird. After plucking its feathers, I eat it raw. The food strengthens me and I resolve to follow a small stream to its end. This isn't far but given my condition and the thickness of the undergrowth, it takes the afternoon. The stream brings me to another small lake. Here I spend the night. The next day I circle the lake, looking for another stream but there is no other stream. I have no choice but to plunge into the woods and hope that I will somehow find a way out. I make no attempt to move softly but crash noisily through underbrush and over fallen logs. If there are bears close by, I want them to hear me. Bogodorasook says most black bears will run if they hear you coming. I do not know how long I blunder through the forest in this way. I have become wilder than the animals and forget I am a man. When I eventually stumble into a clearing where a dead bear lies on the ground, I am amazed it is the bear who lies there and not myself. I am so crazed that I imagine I am the bear and that it is me who is lying on the ground.

Then I feel something sharp against my skin. I look down and see a spear pointed at my chest. Such is my wretchedness that I look not at the man holding the weapon, but at the end of the spear. I notice how sharp the stone point is. I think how cleanly it could enter my flesh and pierce my heart. Is it because I am dead that I am not afraid? The spear is held steady and high. My gaze follows the holder's arm until it reaches his face. The face is familiar. I search my thoughts for his name. Zathrasook. I begin to laugh. How strange it is that Zathrasook is still the hunter and I am the hunted. Zathrasook lowers his spear. Then I notice Tisewsut standing close by.

I don't know what Zathrasook and Tisewsut saw when they looked at me, but from what was said later around the camp-fire, what they saw was not the beast I felt myself to be but a wild man with twigs in his hair, a face scratched and spotted with bites, clothes torn and ragged, a human arm crusted and swollen.

"Wobee!"

Was that Zathrasook or Tisewsut?

Zathrasook, I think, for I remember him saying, "You're a hard man to get rid of, Wobee. I suppose now that we've found you, we'll have to take you back."

I wasn't tied or carried. Instead the bear was tied to a pole. I stumbled after Zathrasook and Tisewsut as they carried the bear out of the woods to the shore. After the bear was put in the canoe, I lay on its fur and was paddled across the bay to our camp.

Imamasduit cleaned my wound and covered it with spruce gum. She gave me warm broth and told me to rest. I slept for days. After I recovered and my arm had healed, four of us went to the ship cove and brought back the canoe which was where I had hidden it beneath the alders. I left the rune stone where it was.

Many days after my return, when we were getting ready to move inland to our winter camp, Imamasduit handed me the calendar stick I had set aside during the Summer and forgotten. As I took the stick, I saw sorrow in her eyes, a sadness that came from the fact that I had disappointed her. I took the stick to the water's edge and threw it with my good arm as far as I could into the sea.

Now that the caribou season is over, I spend long hours with the Osweet inside our winter mamateek. Mandshet has become a lusty, lively baby who often makes us laugh. Soon there will be another baby, for Adensit is far gone with child. There have been other changes as well. Although Zathrasook is now friendly toward me and Abidith goes out of her way to be kind, Imamasduit and Bogodorasook are not as welcoming as they had been before. Because they stood by me when others were unfriendly, they find it harder to forget my betrayal of them. Nor can I forget the picture of them wakening one morning to find the new canoe and myself gone. Just as my mother, father, sister and brothers have had to live with my absence, so too have Imamasduit and Bogodorasook had to live with empty places I have made. It will take time and effort to regain their trust. In the meantime I do whatever tasks are needed to keep our family alive and strong. And I carve. I have carved a needlecase for Imamasduit and three bone arrowheads for Bogodorasook. I took my time with these carvings, wanting to put my care and respect for the old ones into my gifts. Every so often I reach into the pouch where I keep the Creator's stone and take out the comb I once carved for Abidith. Because wood is forgiving, I have been able to alter the picture in such a way that the ship has been made into a canoe. I have also scraped away the mast. In its place I am carving the figure of a young woman standing in the canoe, a woman who looks at me with a clear, unfaltering gaze. I am in no hurry to finish the comb, knowing it will be a long time before our next summer gathering beside the western sea. When that time comes, I will seek out Ahune and give her the comb.

Author's Note

Although this story comes from the writer's imagination and is entirely a work of fiction, it was written around archaeological and historical facts. One of these is that Greenlanders and Icelanders, Leif Eiriksson chief among them, came to northern Newfoundland early in the 1000s and built Leifsbudir in a place now known as L'Anse aux Meadows. Archaeological evidence supports the likelihood that the ancestors of the Beothuk were living in northern Newfoundland around that time. The precursors of the Inuit came and went in this area as well. According to the Icelandic sagas, there were several occasions when the Norse and the aboriginal people came in contact with each other.

Centuries later, as Europeans came in greater numbers to Newfoundland to live, contact between them and the aboriginal people increased. By the 1700s, the Beothuk were the main aboriginal group living in

Newfoundland. As the Europeans settled along the coast, the Beothuks moved inland in order to avoid them.

During this period, several Beothuks were abducted by white people. (The reverse also occurred.) In 1791, Oubee, a young Beothuk girl, was abducted during a raid on a Beothuk camp in the Bay of Exploits. For a time Oubee lived with a white family in Trinity Bay. Two years later she was taken by them to England, where she died shortly thereafter.

Shawnadithit, the last of the Beothuk—the red ochre people—died in St. John's in 1829.

No one knows how many like Oubee were abducted between Leif Eiriksson's arrival in Newfoundland and Shawnadithit's premature death.

Joan Clark
St. John's, Newfoundland

Acknowledgments

I would like to thank people who read various drafts of this novel and made helpful suggestions: Anne Hart, Tony Clark, Pamela Kuryluk, Gillian Lester, Nora Lester and Margaret Macmillan. I would also like to thank Birgitta Wallace, Martha Drake, Susan Maunder, Ingeborg Marshall and Robert McGhee for providing me with information useful to the novel. I also appreciate the co-operation of the Newfoundland Museum and the Centre for Newfoundland Studies, Memorial University. I am particularly grateful to Ralph Pastore who read the story for archaeological and historical accuracy; I thank him for his sound advice. Again I am indebted to Cynthia Good for her enthusiasm and guiding hand.